**NO SAFE HOUSE**

To Alanna
with much
love
Diane

# NO SAFE HOUSE

## DIANE POULIN

*Signature*
EDITIONS

Cover design by Terry Gallagher/Doowah Design.
Cover photo of Diane Poulin by Mike McKenna.
Printed and bound in Canada by AGMV Marquis Imprimeur.

We acknowledge the support of The Canada Council for the Arts and the Manitoba Arts Council for our publishing program.

**National Library of Canada Cataloguing in Publication**

Poulin, Diane, 1958-
          No safe house / Diane Poulin.

ISBN 0-921833-93-8

          I. Title.

PS8581.O839N6 2003          C813'.6          C2003-906147-7

Signature Editions, P.O. Box 206, RPO Corydon
Winnipeg, Manitoba, R3M 3S7

It seems the more eyes we grow, the less we see...

# CHAPTER 1

Jill and Phoebe are crouching over the metal grate, fingers sliding into the small holes, pulling at it. The concrete basement floor is cold under their hands and knees.

"Here." Jill gives it a final yank, almost tumbling backwards as the metal clangs free. "Pass the stuff."

Phoebe is leaning forward, looking down the sewer into the empty black hole. Her blonde ponytail slides over her shoulder, almost touching the floor. She picks up one piece of the mouldy bread piled on the basement floor, and drops it in.

Jill leans in too, so she can hear the soft swoosh as it hits water, somewhere down there. She giggles nervously, as she always does when they are flirting with trouble.

"You take some of them," Phoebe says, passing her half the stack. It almost makes them gag, pulling the green-black bread out of the waxed paper wrappings. It's like crusty socks at the bottom of a locker, discovered days after gym class. They are shoving them faster and faster down the sewer. These sandwiches aren't really sandwiches at all. They are just two pieces of bread with a hint of margarine in between. Jill carries them to and from school each day in her lunch box, and simply does not eat them. She won't even open her lunch box, because the bread is so foreign in its pure black ryeness. Her mother is not from here, she wasn't born here like Jill, and she's the one who insists this dry, hard junk is bread. All the other kids at school eat clean, white slices, or light brown sandwiches with peanut butter and baloney and Cheez Whiz inside. Jill's stack of stinking, moulding bread at the back of her bedroom closet has been her secret for weeks, and it's making her panicky when her mother comes into her room. It is her best friend Phoebe who comes up with the idea of sinking the black bread down the hole.

Phoebe is almost twelve years old and Jill is close to thirteen. It's late May, and they want to be outside.

Jill wrestles the metal grate back in place. Each day, for the rest of the school year, she will come down here before her mother gets home from work and dump her bread. Jill is tall and skinny, with thin brown hair tied back from her bony face.

"Let's get out of here," Phoebe says, her eye catching the woman in the corner as she straightens. It always gives her a start, that mannequin, propped up against the cement wall, with its blank eye sockets and white face. Jill's mother tells the children she is a fashion designer, but really her job is cutting cloth at a garment factory downtown. They call her Bea. It makes her feel too old when she's called Mother, or Mom. Here, in the basement, Bea creates her own clothes, at a long wooden work table. Today there is a bolt of electric blue unfurled on the table. The mannequin is naked. Jill told her once the mannequin is exactly like Bea, cool and slippery to the touch. It is always dark and echoey down here, with nothing more than the lumbering furnace throwing shadows. It gives Phoebe the creeps.

The girls run up the wooden steps, and across the shining linoleum floor in the kitchen. Jill puts her lunch box on the counter, catches Phoebe's hand, and they grin. Mission accomplished.

Delores opens her bedroom door down the hall.

"What are you doing?" she asks.

"None of your beeswax," Jill says. Delores is only seven, and Jill mostly ignores her younger sister.

Delores takes the same hard bread sandwich to school every day and eats it. As soon as her lunch box is empty, she looks for things to take so she can fill it up. She steals paper clips and apples and staplers and chalk. She eats whatever she can, even the soft, gummy erasers. The rest she hides, mainly in her room, under her bed, and in the cracks in her closet floor.

"We're going out," Jill calls, and they slam the front door. Jill makes her way home from school every day with the cool steel key slapping against her chest, on the string around her neck. Bea says not to tell people that they are alone, don't let on. Phoebe thinks this is great. She lives down at the other end of the street, ten houses away, and her mother is always around when she comes flying in from school to dump her books. Like now.

Janice Currie is outside sweeping cobwebs from the corners of her living room window. She cups her hands to her mouth and calls out to her daughter.

"Phoebe." She motions with her arm. "Come here."

Phoebe glides up the paved driveway with Jill in tow. Janice sees how they balance impatiently on their bikes, anxious to be off.

"Hold your horses," she says. "I just thought you might want a snack." Jill looks quickly at Phoebe, ready to get off her bike, but Phoebe shakes her head no.

"Later. We gotta go now, Mom." Phoebe pushes off, barely glancing back, knowing Jill will follow her lead.

"Okay. Come in and get something when your bike ride is done." Janice shades her eyes from the late afternoon sun, watching the two of them careen down the driveway and back out onto Glendale Avenue.

"Let's go to the graveyard," Jill says, and they swing left, best friends heading out, bursts of lilacs rolling over them as they bike past the mowed and clipped front lawns. On bad days, when the wind blows strong from the southeast, the rotting smell from the slaughterhouse settles over Oakwood. No one hangs laundry outside and Phoebe and Jill know they have to turn their backs. But today it is the smell of lilacs, not pigs, colouring the air.

"Hey, girls," Laurel Murray calls as they pass her red brick house. Laurel is sitting on her front step. Phoebe and Jill barely acknowledge her. There is no reason to, she's old even if they do call her Laurel instead of Mrs. Murray, and her kids are too young for them to play with.

Laurel sighs. She's twenty-five years old. No one in the neighbourhood is sure about that because since she arrived here last year she's told different stories. She tells Phoebe's mother she is twenty-seven and she tells others, like Gary and Madeline next door, that she's thirty. When she says she's thirty she adds that she is a dental technician who quit working to raise her children. She stands up to go inside, frowning at the incessant barking of a dog nearby. This neighbourhood is full of dogs; she can't stand it some days, like now, when there is no one around to talk to.

Laurel wears her Levi's jeans snug, with a T-shirt tucked in. Her brown hair is flecked with gold, exactly like her eyes. She's good-looking, and she knows it. Not that it matters. She's stuck here baking an angel food cake, with three kids napping, most of the time bored out of her mind. Laurel can speed-read a book a day and possesses the raw intelligence to absorb and recall almost everything. These days she doesn't bother reading much late at night. No one to impress here, is what she thinks most of the time. Gary next door is an excellent diversion, although not for discussing books.

She steps over the clutter of toys and sweaters in her hallway to get to the kitchen, where the oven timer is beeping. As she's grabbing for mitts to get the cake out, she hears the car next door pulling into the driveway, the crunch of gravel and the slamming door, the hearty "Hi, I'm home."

"It just figures," Laurel says out loud in her kitchen. She timed this all wrong, and now Gary is already in his house, without exchanging one word. This is one of the highlights of her day, snatched away, just like that. Laurel slaps her cake down onto the wire rack to cool.

—

Jill pokes Phoebe in the ribs.

"Let's go to The Witch's house," she says. They slow down in front of the two-storey, wooden house. Ivy shoots out fingers and clutches the peeling paint. With its overgrown bushes and scraggly oaks, this place is like a forest in the midst of the manicured yards. It smells damp and cool.

"Good idea." Phoebe nods her agreement, and they veer left, down the back lane to the broken board in the fence, where they drop their bikes and slither in.

Jill scrapes her legs but keeps inching forward on her belly. Phoebe is already stationed in their spot, behind the bleeding hearts.

"We didn't bring the book," Phoebe says. "We need to remember it all. Look, she's near the window."

They wiggle closer together, making their bodies like grass, flat against the earth.

The book forgotten under Phoebe's bed is a spiral, lined notebook. It's where they record the results of their spying. It is filled with license plate numbers, the whereabouts of people in Oakwood at different times of the day, descriptions of strangers. But pages and pages are devoted to this house, and the woman inside it. The Witch, maybe the good kind, maybe not. You can never be sure. The adults call her The Walker, among other things.

"She's looking this way," Jill whispers.

"No, she's not. Shhh," Phoebe whispers back.

They see the drapes flutter, and the shadow move and glint behind the window.

"Remember this," Jill prods. "It's your turn to put it in the book."

The woman inside sees the girls crouched outside in her bushes. It has been almost a week since she's watched them, watching her. She decides to make it worth their while today. She picks up the floor mat in front of her kitchen sink. She edges her way to the back door, counts to ten, and then flings it open. She's flapping her arms, shaking the mat, looking around wildly.

Jill jumps up shrieking and going right into her high-pitched giggle as Phoebe grabs her arm, dragging them towards the fence. Her heart is pounding. They will never make it back under the fence. That's too slow. In a split second she sizes up their chances of escape and starts bolting for the thick bushes at the side of the house.

"Run, run, run," she's chanting to Jill, who always trips behind Phoebe when they are in a panic.

The Witch gives the mat a good whack and goes back into her house.

The girls are fighting their way through the brambles on the side of the house, branches slapping up against tender skin, half blind with the urgent need to get away. The bushes leave marks on them, red welts on a thigh, arm, back of the knee. Finally they make it to the safety of the back lane, jump onto their waiting bikes, and head towards Phoebe's house.

"Close call," Phoebe pants. "I think she saw you."

"Did not," Jill wheezes.

They slow down now, passing the old Warbanskis, sitting on their hard kitchen chairs on their front stoop. They pass the house where all the teenage boys hang out, where Tom lives, usually one of their prime spy locations but also the most difficult. They make their way down Glendale Avenue, past Phoebe's aunt and uncle's house, and then finally, still slightly winded, they are on their own turf.

"So where did you go?" Phoebe's mother asks, as they barrel through the kitchen on their way to Phoebe's room upstairs.

"Nowhere," Phoebe says.

"Not far," Jill adds.

"You sure look like you've seen a ghost," her mother says. "Lemonade?"

"Yes," both girls say. "Please," Jill remembers to tack on.

"Can we take it to my room? We have something important we have to do," Phoebe tries.

"No. Sit here and drink." Phoebe's mother is pouring them tall glasses, setting them down on the kitchen table.

Reluctantly, Phoebe shrugs into a chair and Jill follows. Jill is staring at the bowl of fruit in the middle of the table.

"Have a banana," Phoebe's mother says, noticing the hungry look, pushing the bowl towards Jill.

"Ugh, no," Phoebe says, but Jill's hand snakes out and grabs and peels almost in one motion. Furtively. Jill is hungry. She did not eat lunch today. Jill usually shares Phoebe's sandwich at school since they started stuffing her bread down the sewer. But today Phoebe was chosen as a monitor during the lunch hour and so they did not eat together. Jill is teaching herself how to control hunger pangs, how to get past the clawing she feels in her stomach.

Phoebe's mother watches to see the colour in their cheeks return, the pinched whiteness receding, their breathing even out.

"So where have you been?" she asks casually, as if it doesn't matter in the least, leaning her hip against the kitchen counter.

Jill and Phoebe exchange quick, guilty glances, trying to decide what to say.

Phoebe looks into her lemonade glass. "Climbing trees," she says, knowing her mother would have already spotted the scratches on their arms and legs. Her mother narrows her eyes, decides to let it go, for now.

"Well, it sure made you thirsty."

"Yeah," Phoebe agrees quickly. "Thanks, Mom." She's moving, tugging Jill by the arm, and they get away for the second time in less than an hour.

———

Two of Laurel's three children are awake, needing apple juice. Kayla is five, and Jamie is three. Laurel seats them at the counter, with animal crackers and juice, watching the clock. At exactly twenty-eight minutes after four, she goes to her picture living room window, and waits. "Shush for a minute, I'm busy," she calls back to her kids, who are trying to ask her questions, not liking it when she is out of the room. "Just hush for one minute."

There she is.

The Walker comes out of her house, dressed, as always, in her yellow plastic raincoat that stops at mid-thigh, like a child's. She has on her baggy pants, and Nike running shoes. Her stringy brown hair is pulled back with an elastic band. When she gets to the end of her driveway, she turns to the right, as always, staring straight ahead and down slightly, as though her gaze is a headlight on a car, needing to stay focused ten feet ahead.

The Walker walks. She goes in circles, three times a day, clockwise. That's three hours a day, morning, afternoon, and evening, round and round the neighbourhood.

Laurel leans against her window, knuckles pressed against her mouth. This is the most distressing part of her day. When her husband Brian gets home she almost always mentions it.

"She's still at it," she'll say.

"Who?" Brian will look up from the paper, or the TV, preoccupied.

"Walking. Her, she's still going in her circles," Laurel will say.

"She's not hurting anyone," Brian says mildly.

"It's easy for you to say. You're off at work. You don't have to actually see her every single day." Laurel's voice starts to rise. The Walker hovers near the edge of her mind. Laurel feels brainwashed sometimes, as though The Walker is doing it precisely for this reason, to have this exact impact on Laurel.

"It's driving me crazy," she snaps at her husband. "This whole neighbourhood drives me crazy." Brian picks up his newspaper and leaves the room, as he always does when Laurel gets like this.

Brian can tune out The Walker and the barking dogs and three kids banging pots and pans. This is his talent.

At this moment, before her husband arrives home from his job selling breeding sows for the hog companies, Laurel leans against her window.

The Walker does not vary her stride; it is not fast, not slow. Sometimes the neighbourhood children ride half a block behind her on their bicycles, round and round, following her just because. But not today. She strides past the Ukrainian couple, still on their front stoop. Joseph Warbanski looks away every time The Walker passes in front of his home. He shares the opinion of the children: she is a Witch.

When The Walker reaches the house at the end of the street, Phoebe's mother, out sweeping the driveway now, looks up.

"Hello, Margaret," she calls out. Janice is the only person in the neighbourhood who speaks to The Walker whenever she sees her. She is the only person who bothered to find out her name, which she did by questioning the letter carrier. Must be two years ago now, Janice thinks, as she sees the yellow jacket swinging by for the thousandth time.

"Oh, she gets mail all right," the mailman told her.

"Some people in the neighbourhood think she's a bit of an odd duck," Phoebe's mother said. "You know, the way she just appeared in the night, after Lillian died like that."

"That right?" the mailman answers. The Walker is a favourite client of his because her house is easy, no cats, no dogs, the sidewalk always shoveled in winter. That's all he cares about.

"What's her name?" Phoebe's mother had asked.

"Mail says Margaret Sutherland."

Janice had not wanted to appear too nosy, so it took a few chats with the mailman, over the course of several weeks, to learn that Margaret received parcels of all shapes and sizes from Boston, New York, Toronto, and Los Angeles. It was unusual for a woman living alone in this solidly working class neighbourhood in Winnipeg to get so many packages, so of course even the mailman had noticed. He had no idea what was inside them. Once, he tried to ask her, jokingly, when Margaret was signing for a delivery. She looked right at him, something she never did normally, and that look was piercing. No answering humour in her eyes, so he had dropped it. The boxes keep arriving.

Now that Janice knows her name she calls out hello when Margaret passes. Janice has also learned, over the past two years, that Margaret was Lillian's only niece, and when the old spinster died, she left the house on Glendale Avenue and all its furnishings to Margaret. The Walker simply slid into the neighbourhood, without moving vans or fanfare, without children or pets or introductions. Just slid in, and started her rounds.

Janice watches now as Margaret Sutherland, neighbourhood Walker, keeps going, veering right for the first dip in her circle at Phoebe's house, never looking over at Janice, not answering her greeting.

Inside, at the window, Phoebe also spots The Witch and is reciting the inventory to Jill. Jill is taking notes.

"I think her socks are grey. She's wearing the red hair band today."

"Go slower."

"I can't. Write faster. My mother is trying to talk to her," she reports, groaning, and both girls roll their eyes at how dumb adults can be. They know you don't try to exchange recipes with a witch.

They know she does not bake, or get stains out of carpets, or pull weeds in her front lawn. Phoebe's mother wants to believe she does do these things, but Jill and Phoebe know better. They would have notes on this if she did them. She does other things.

Phoebe has overheard her mother saying to her father that the poor woman Margaret just needs some friends and a chance to fit in. She actually sent Phoebe down the street last summer to invite The Witch to the annual neighbourhood barbecue and block party. Phoebe had grabbed Jill, and they had made it to the front of her house, looking up at the long windows through the trees. No way they were knocking on her door. They told Phoebe's mother she did not want to come to the barbecue. That was the truth, anyway, she wouldn't want to.

"I think she goes flying on that kitchen mat at night," Jill says.

"To the woods, I'll bet," Phoebe adds.

"To make brews."

"To meet other witches."

"Should I put that in the book?" Jill wants to know. They usually stick to facts that they see, because that is what real spies do. They've never actually seen her flying, and it's the first time they've seen her shaking that kitchen mat.

"Hmm. Yeah, put it in, but write it in a different colour," Phoebe decides. She's searching through the top drawer of her desk. She finds a pen with green ink.

"Perfect. This is perfect," Jill says, starting a new page about The Witch in green ink.

"Girls," Phoebe's mother is at the bottom of the stairs. "Jill's mother will be home soon."

"Okay," Phoebe calls down.

"Come with me." Jill demands this, quick and urgent.

Phoebe knows why. She shrugs. "Yeah."

"I'm just walking Jill home," Phoebe says to her mother. She half wishes her mother would say no, you can't, supper is almost ready. They can smell the huge pot of spaghetti sauce bubbling slowly on the back burner.

But Phoebe's mother does not say that.

"Okay, sweetie. Don't be long," is all she says.

The girls head back down the street. The sky now is like the weak tea Phoebe's mother drinks. The trees, bushes and grass are doused in a yellow wash and even the old Warbanskis look soft around the edges as Jill and Phoebe pass.

"Too late," Jill says, darting a quick look at Phoebe. They can see Bea is already in the house. She's just arrived home. It usually went better if Jill and Phoebe were there first, pretending to read books.

Jill goes up the front stairs.

"Left her here alone, I see," Bea says. She opens the screen door, and yanks Jill by the arm, pulling her into the house.

"Phoebe forgot her book," Jill says, and her voice is already going squeaky, her cold fingers clutching at Phoebe.

Jill is pulling Phoebe in as her mother pulls her in.

Bea has her high heel in her hand, and as soon as the screen door closes, she swings, and the heel connects with Jill's shin. One short, sharp jab to the thin bone. That bruise will be purple. It does not slow Jill down. She's darting past Bea, towards her room, dragging Phoebe.

They make it into the room.

It's one of those days, they can see with a glance at Bea. She has that cold fury in her face and there is no bag of groceries in her arms. Jill knows things did not go well with Bea's boss Mr. Findley because if they had, extra groceries would appear. Tonight they will eat one boiled egg for dinner, with more awful black bread. Bea makes them eat the eggshells. She says that's the best part, where all the protein is, but no one else Jill knows eats eggshells for supper and the crunching hurts her teeth. Food in this house is erratic and controlled by Bea. It hurts to chew here, Jill thinks. Not like over at Phoebe's, where everything is soft and within reach and rich with flavour.

Delores stands at her bedroom door, watching, as Bea stalks down the hall.

Jill is moving quickly, scrambling over her bed to the crack between the mattress and the wall. She's wedging herself in, with Phoebe in front of her, ready. As ready as she can get. She's learned, by trial and error, that this is the best position.

Bea is in the room, her shoe in her hand.

Phoebe watches her, crouched next to her best friend. Her heart pounds now, waiting, and sometimes she feels like bursting into laughter. Phoebe knows it's wrong, but she can feel it welling up inside her so strongly she has to bite the inside of her cheek.

Bea's legs are wrapped in black stockings and her frilly, short skirt floats in swirls of blue and green. She sews her clothes at night in the basement, carefully dressing the mannequin with designs she copies from the London and Paris magazines she buys downtown. Bea is painfully thin, like the models on TV. She wears four-inch heels and in the winter her boots lace up her thighs. That's how she dresses, in a neighbourhood of women in stretch slacks and long, loose blouses.

It's Bea's face that Phoebe and Jill watch.

It's hidden, as always, behind pancake make-up. Bea glues on false eyelashes and pencils in a make-believe mole above her right eye. Her hair is dyed auburn, teased and sprayed, sometimes in a twist, usually, like now, free to her shoulders. On good days, the girls watch her apply this face, fascinated, and are rewarded with little bits of powder brushes across their skin, their choice of lipstick. Bea always wears lipstick, and even though she carefully makes her mouth larger, Phoebe can see the real lips are thinned now, and hard.

She reaches out and grabs Phoebe's arm, pulling her away from Jill.

"Move," she tells Phoebe. "Get your book and go home."

"No, she has to help me with my homework," Jill tries. "I don't know the page numbers."

This delaying tactic is straight habit on Jill's part. It does not make any difference in the end, but Jill keeps believing it will.

Bea is swinging the high-heeled shoe again, down on Jill's fingers which are still clutching Phoebe's shirt. Jill's fingers lose their grip, curling into her palm.

With a quick glance over her shoulder, Phoebe starts to move away from Jill. Jill nods, knowing Phoebe cannot shield her, feeling better just having her in the room.

Jill raises her arms to protect her face.

Her mother hits her on the shoulder, the hip, wherever she can reach with Jill wedged so tight against the wall. It is quiet and efficient; it does not take long, three or four good hits that connect, and then the lips start to slacken. Phoebe, huddled near the bedroom closet watching, knows it is over for now.

Jill occasionally grunts, but she does not cry. She will have two welts, and two bruises. She will pretend she has a stomach ache to get out of gym class, so no one will see.

Delores has gone back into her room and closed the door. She is chewing on a key that she found. She is developing the ability to crumble and chew and swallow metal. It will take Delores one week to eat this key in its entirety.

These are some of the facts Phoebe and Jill do not write in their spy book.

# CHAPTER 2

Laurel is humming, standing on her back steps hanging laundry on the line, the sun soft on her face. Kayla and Jamie are playing with their red pails and shovels in the sandbox and baby Andrea is napping in her carriage under the tree. At this moment, Laurel is so content, she pauses to inhale it.

Laurel hangs laundry in a deliberate manner. First she pegs the socks, toes first, then the underwear. When she gets to shirts, she fishes in the basket item by item, pulling out dark colours in a graduated fashion, the shades going from black to white. Prints and patterns go after. Pants hang from their bottoms, not their waistbands. Sheets get pegged last, billowing closest to the house, so they won't get tangled in the oak tree in the centre of the yard. A perfectly hung clothesline, smelling like a summer breeze and creaking gently, makes Laurel feel safe, and loved.

She is sitting under the tree, relaxing, rocking the baby carriage with her foot, watching her boy and girl play, when Gary comes out onto his back deck next door.

"Hello," he says cheerfully.

"Hello yourself. Home from work today?"

"I just took a couple of hours off," he says, moving to lean his elbows on top of the back fence. "I'm building the loft for the next couple of weeks so I'm going to order the lumber today." Gary keeps his voice affable, the friendly neighbour next door who's always out chatting to people on the corner, walking his German shepherd. But his eyes move over Laurel in her short shorts, and she knows it.

"Would you like to come over for coffee?" she asks, raising an eyebrow so it's a challenge.

"Yeah," he says, moving to the back gate.

"Gary, Gary, Gary." Kayla is up, out of her sandbox, clamouring around his legs for attention, lifting her arms. He obligingly swings Kayla, and then Jamie needs a turn. He's happy to play with the kids while Laurel is inside, making coffee. He's had coffee midday like this with Janice Currie before, when Gordon was at work. This is what he is telling himself. It's all perfectly normal neighbourliness.

When Laurel pushes open the screen door with her hip, coffee tray laden with cups and Kool Aid for the kids, he can see she has changed her blouse. Laurel has put on a tight-fitting sleeveless top, the kind teenagers wear sauntering around the mall.

"Okay kids, you take your Kool Aid and cookies to the picnic table. Gary and I are having coffee now. Stop pestering him, Kayla."

She gets them settled a few feet away with treats and a colouring book. When she leans over to kiss the top of Jamie's head in quick affection, she catches Gary's eye. He does not look away.

Laurel makes sure her hand lingers on Gary's when she passes him his cup of coffee. She looks at him in the slanting way she uses with men to let them know, and they always get the message. Laurel can get on a bus, chat for a few minutes with the driver, and go anywhere in the city for free. Clerks in government departments, overworked and sullen in their cubicles, find a way to help Laurel when she needs her water turned on, or a document explained, or a phone hooked up.

It's the look of promise she tosses out so easily. Laurel turns this on and off at will. She has the careless attraction of someone who always expects to have a man in her back pocket and usually does. She leans over to offer Gary a cookie.

Gary is at least fifteen years older than Laurel, a hard-working man with a hard body. He has two teenage sons and has been married to Madeline for twenty years. He's always been faithful, not because that's the rule, but because that's the way he wants it. He intends to keep it that way. Gary is telling himself that any man would be looking at an attractive young woman like Laurel and flirting a little. That's all he is doing.

"The roof will come off tomorrow. Weather forecast is good so I'll be working straight through the next few days. I hope the noise won't disturb you."

"Hmm," she says. "I like being disturbed." Deliberately, she holds his eyes with hers.

Gary is shifting in his chair. He breathes deeply, and looks away from the tilting eyes, the sandal swinging from a slender ankle.

"Thanks for the coffee," he says, turning his body away, getting up to leave.

"Is Madeline on holidays, too, next week?" Laurel asks.

"Yes," he says.

"Then she'll be around?"

"Yes."

"Too bad," Laurel says. This is the farthest she has gone with Gary to let him know she is available. She leans back, and waits.

"Mom, he's cheating," Kayla shrieks and tries swatting Jamie.

"Am not, am not, am not," Jamie pipes in and starts struggling down from the picnic table, incensed.

Gary does not answer Laurel. He crosses to the picnic table, but Kayla doesn't want him, she wants Laurel's undivided attention and so she shrieks louder. Gary gets out of the Murrays' back yard without looking directly at Laurel again.

—

Phoebe is tearing into the house, dropping school books onto the living room chair, already unbuttoning her good school blouse so she can get into her T-shirt and out again.

"Hello to you, too," her mother calls after her.

"Jill and I are going bike riding," she calls back from her room.

"How about, may Jill and I go bike riding?" her mother prompts.

"Yeah," Jill agrees.

"Homework?"

"Just a bit. Easy stuff. I'll do it after supper," Phoebe says, bounding down the stairs.

"Well, take these apples. And a couple of juices," her mother says.

"Thanks. See ya." Phoebe is stuffing the food into her pockets, screen door slamming behind her, wheeling her bike to the road.

Jill is already waiting for her to arrive, straddling her bike and tapping one foot impatiently as Phoebe swings into her driveway.

"Here," Jill hands over an apple and a juice box.

"Thanks," Jill says. Her brow furrows for a second. "Hang on." She jumps off the bike and takes the steps two at a time, banging on the front door because she does not want to waste time fishing out her key.

Delores appears, cracking open the door.

"You aren't supposed to answer the door, stupid," Jill says.

"I knew it was you," Delores replies.

Jill shoves the apple into her hands, spins on her heel and runs back to Phoebe. She punctures the juice box with the mini-straw and gulps it down quickly. Delores, she knows, will chew that whole apple, core, seeds and all.

"Okay, let's go."

"Where?"

"I dunno."

"The Nest," Phoebe says, already pedaling in the direction of the graveyard.

"Yeah, good," Jill agrees.

They enter the graveyard by the back gate, and ride in the loop that leads them to the river. At the back corner of the cemetery, Jill and Phoebe have created The Nest.

They swing their bikes behind the tall row of hedges that ring the graveyard, carefully concealing them from view. They head to the last clump of bushes, where there's a small opening at its base. Getting down on all fours, the girls squeeze through the narrow entrance. Now they are inside a leafy cave, high enough to sit up in and long enough to lie down in. The dense branches keep out the rain and sun, but enough light filters through to read or write in their book. Jill and Phoebe discovered this fort by accident last summer, while kicking a ball half-heartedly. It had rolled right to this opening. A fort abandoned by other children already into adolescence, too old for secret places in the graveyard. Overgown, somewhat, but just waiting for Jill and Phoebe.

"So what do you want to do now?" Jill asks, leaning on her elbow.

Phoebe settles onto her back, looking at the broken light shifting above her.

"Pass me a comic."

Jill reaches behind her, riffles through their stack, and passes one to Phoebe. She rolls onto her stomach, finding an action comic she knows almost by heart, and starts to read.

Inside The Nest, Jill and Phoebe have playing cards, comics, a bottle of musk oil to keep the mosquitoes away; Delores had stolen the musk oil from the janitor's closet at school and Jill had forced her to hand it over. They have the old grey picnic blanket taken from Phoebe's rec room, crayons and markers, and their newest addition, a bag of shiny marbles. They also have a pile of rocks for weapons. Inside The Nest they can lean on their elbows and see the graveyard's dirt road through a few carefully yanked holes in the bottom, and they can watch the river, just in case. Just in case anyone comes looking for them by boat, that is. Like pirates. Jill and Phoebe tried to keep their secret place operating all year, but in winter the graveyard closes at dusk and the gates are locked by the time school is out because it's already dark. They tried coming here on a January Saturday but by the time they had pushed their way through the snow, fattened in their layers of sweaters and jackets and mitts, they had barely fit inside and there was nothing to do, with their supplies all packed away under Phoebe's bed. And so The Nest has become even more special, because it's their secret summer spot.

———

The phone is ringing just as Laurel is heading into the kitchen to see what is in the fridge for supper.

"I'm going to be home late," Brian says.

"Working?" asks Laurel.

"Yes. How are the kids?"

"Fine. Well, not great, the baby is teething and cranky."

"Teeth. Awesome things." Brian is smiling.

"Looks that way. Listen, Brian, I was thinking I could use some help this summer with the kids. School is just about out now and I thought maybe Jill and Phoebe could be mother's helpers. We wouldn't have to pay them too much."

"Who?"

"You know, the two little girls who are always around on their bikes, not so little actually. They will be babysitting our kids in a year or two."

There's quiet for a minute on the other end of the line.

"You mean we will still be living here in a couple of years?" Brian asks carefully.

"Of course we will," Laurel says firmly, but unconsciously her eyes glance out her kitchen window, to Gary and Madeline's house.

"Sure," Brian says. He has learned to walk softly around his wife. He knows her better than she knows herself. When she starts making plans for them to stay somewhere, long-term, it is a sign that Laurel is getting restless. High-strung is what the last doctor called her, back in Saskatchewan. That was when she got caught shoplifting at Zellers, stuffing cosmetics and, of all things, cans of tuna into her diaper bag. Brian shifts the phone under his chin and writes a note to himself on his notepad. Check out the management program.

"What?"

"Sure, get the girls to help out. It'll be good for the kids to get used to them," Brian says.

"Okay, that's what I thought. I'll talk to them today. See you later."

"And Laurel?" he says.

"Hmm?"

"Love you."

"Oh, me too," she says, but hangs up quickly.

Brian stares at the phone in his hand, shakes his head. One year they have lived in Oakwood, that's all, long enough for Andrea to come into the world and Kayla to start school. He shakes his head again. More potential to keep moving around if he goes down the management track. He might as well take the intern program the company keeps pushing his way. Brian hangs up the phone.

———

Jill and Phoebe are back on their bikes, heading towards the teenagers' house.

"I think we should leave our bikes at your house," Jill says.

"We can leave them behind the fence. No one will see them."

"We always have to do it your way," Jill accuses.

"We do not."

"Do, too."

Spying on the teenagers is risky business. There is the tree, the vicious dog, and the boys themselves that are all dangerous.

Phoebe relents. "Oh, all right, let's leave the bikes at the beach."

They wheel their bikes in back of the pump house. The beach is not really a beach; it's just a strip of pebbly sand at the river's edge. There are some people in Oakwood, like Anna Warbanski, who remember swimming here, when there were only a few streets and a lot of fields and forest, and Oakwood was like being out in the country. The water was clean then.

Now the beach is a park with grass and beds of marigolds and swings and monkey bars. Children still occasionally squat by the water with colanders trying to scoop up the minnows and tadpoles in the shallows. But those are harder and harder to find, and takes more time than toddlers are willing to spend.

"Throw it," Phoebe says, her voice low.

"One, two, three," Jill raises her arm, and hurls a rock over the fence which is taller than they are, into the teenagers' backyard. They both hold their breath. Okay.

This is how they check to make sure that Baxter the dog is not in the backyard. He's a boxer, with a menacing growl, terrifying teeth, and an unrelenting bark that finds them instantly. Even his eyes are beady, black raisins in folds of skin.

Jill and Phoebe made the mistake, in their early spy days, of underestimating Baxter. They'd climbed into the tree and the dog zoomed directly towards them, snapping at the tree trunk, trapping them. It was a good thing the teenagers had not been home that day, because Jill and Phoebe would have been discovered. They'd had to wait out the dog, clutching the tree branch, until Tom's father came home from work and called Baxter to the back door.

Tom is the teenager who lives there, most of the time, anyway. He lives with his father all week, and his mother on weekends, a few streets away. They followed him one Friday night, because he always kept disappearing, so that's how they know where he goes on weekends. They wrote it down in the section of their book reserved for Teenagers.

"It's your turn to go first." Jill pushes Phoebe.

"I know," she bristles. She's not stalling. She's getting ready.

She reaches down and unlaces her running shoes, strips off her socks, tucks them into a bush in the back lane. You have to do this fence barefoot. There are small knotholes and that's the only grip for fingers and toes, and there is no avoiding the splinters. They have to be endured.

Phoebe grunts as she hoists herself up the fence, wincing at a banged knee, a torn thumb. This is the hardest part, and the scariest. She reaches for a branch. Good, she has it.

"Okay?" Jill whispers from below.

Phoebe grunts again. She has a ledge only a few inches wide to perch on at the top of the fence, and from here she needs to swing herself, clinging to the branch, into the body of the tree. It's important to hit the tree exactly at its crotch, where two thick branches are capable of holding two girls, or else it's a mad shimmy up the trunk and way more scrapes.

Phoebe makes it. Her face splits into a grin.

She gives one short whistle, their signal.

She can hear Jill's heavy breathing, and then her head appears over the fence, her body.

Phoebe reaches out. Whoever goes first helps the second, and the leap is way easier. That's why they trade who has to go first.

Phoebe tugs her hand, and Jill lands half on top of Phoebe, her eyes shining. A perfect execution.

They settle themselves into the top of the tree, behind the leaves. They each have their own branch.

This is hard work, waiting. The girls time this to when high school lets out, but there is no guarantee Tom will come straight home, or bring his friends, or sit in the backyard, or the basement, which they can see. There are no curtains on the basement windows.

Jill is watching a green, fuzzy caterpillar make its way toward some leaves. The birds go silent when Jill and Phoebe arrive, but after a while they forget the girls are there and sing and chatter and hop from branch to branch above them.

Finally the back gate bangs open, startling Phoebe so her heart pounds. Jill and Phoebe's eyes meet through the leaves. It's Tom with Luc and Stretch, so named, the girls know, because he is the shortest kid in the class with no growth spurt in sight. They have the soccer ball with them.

"I'll get some Cokes," Tom says to his friends, kicking shut the back gate.

He unlocks the door to the house with a key he pulls from his pocket.

"Baxter," he's calling. "C'mon boy. What are you doing in the house, anyway? Did Dad put you inside after I left this morning?"

He's bending, trying to scratch behind the dog's ears. Baxter jumps all over his jeans, barking wildly, running to Stretch and back to Tom and then over to Luc.

The friends are kicking the ball, back and forth between them, the dog chasing it.

"Here." Tom throws them each a can of Coke.

The ball rolls to the tree.

Jill looks at Phoebe with wide it-can't-be eyes.

Baxter chases the ball, then suddenly stops barking, tipping his head, sniffing. And now he is crouching, and growling, his teeth like fangs. This is worse than last time because now the teenagers are in the yard and Jill and Phoebe are dead meat for sure.

"Hey, Baxter, cut it out," Tom says.

The dog ignores him.

"Bring the ball, Bax," he tries again.

Baxter does not take his eyes off Phoebe and Jill.

"Dumb dog," Tom says. He walks right to the bottom of the tree, and Phoebe feels like she's going to fall out of her branch, that's how numb her hands are.

"C'mon," Tom says, never glancing up. He kicks the ball, tugs at Baxter's collar. Reluctantly, with a warning glance back over his shoulder in their direction, Baxter follows his master.

Luc, having downed his can of Coke in two gulps, burps.

All three boys laugh.

"Oh yeah?" says Stretch. He belches louder.

"Try this," Tom says. He belches, hits his chest, and belches again, making it a rhythm. The other two copy him, adding variations, and then they move on to farts. Fart, hit the chest, belch. The also fake fart by doing something that only boys seem to master with their armpits. This becomes a three-part harmony, a symphony of guffaws and body noises. Luc, with his cropped, bleached white hair, imagines himself as a rock star. He tells Tom to get his ghetto blaster out here. Tom obligingly hauls out his boom box and now they are synchronizing their farts, burps, hits to a rap hip hop tune, arms flailing, dog singing along.

"Oh, brother." Phoebe risks speaking sideways to Jill. They are making so much noise down there, they'll never catch Jill and Phoebe in their tree now. This is supremely disappointing. Once the possibility of danger is gone there's no real point in being here.

"And now we are stuck," Jill says. "I hope you are happy."

"Me?"

"You're the one who said let's check out the teenagers. I wanted to do The Witch."

"Well. We did The Witch yesterday."

"Well."

All that work, climbing, hiding, and braving the perils, for this. In their book, under the date and the caption Teenagers: Tom, they write one word: Gross.

—

"Wait a minute, Jill, Phoebe. I want to talk to you girls," Laurel calls from her front step. Phoebe and Jill exchange glances, shrug, reluctantly wheel their bikes up the Murrays' driveway.

"I have an idea that would mean some money for you," Laurel says.

"What?" Phoebe asks.

"Sit down. I don't bite." Laurel pats the cement steps, and Jill and Phoebe perch on the edge.

"You know I have three kids," Laurel says, holding Andrea in her lap.

"Yeah," Jill says. She reaches out and lets the baby grab her fingers. Andrea giggles.

"Next year I'll be needing you both to babysit sometimes."

Phoebe squirms. Who cares, she's thinking, that's forever, and this is boring.

"When I was your age," Laurel continues, "I was a mother's helper in the summer. Do you know what that is?"

"No," Jill and Phoebe both say, and Phoebe does not hide the fact that's she's inching towards her bike, anxious to get going.

"Well, I'd be willing to pay you to come here for an hour or two a day and give me a hand doing chores around the house and watching the kids," Laurel says. "Not a lot of money, but enough that you could get chocolate sundaes at the Dairy Queen."

"Yeah?" Jill's eyes light up. Even Phoebe stops fidgeting.

"What would we have to do?" Phoebe asks.

"Maybe take the baby here for a walk in her stroller. Help me pull up the weeds in the garden. Maybe vacuum the living room, or read Kayla a book at her nap time," Laurel says.

"Oh," Phoebe says. None of that sounds particularly thrilling to her.

"Why don't you talk to your parents about it, and I'll check with them tomorrow and see what they have to say?" Laurel adds.

"Okay, thanks." Phoebe recognizes they are free for now, and jumps up, nudging Jill to follow.

When they are safely out of earshot, Phoebe snorts.

"I don't want to do her stupid work," she says.

"I do," Jill says. She wants to eat ice cream all summer. And she thinks Laurel is beautiful, although she does not say this out loud.

"Well," Phoebe says. Usually Jill and Phoebe agree on everything. If Jill is going to do this, then Phoebe pretty much has to or else they will be apart on some of their summer days. That is beyond imagining.

They are now at Phoebe's house.

"Are you coming in?" Phoebe asks.

"Nah. I'll go home, before Bea gets there," Jill says.

"Okay. Bye."

When Phoebe gets into the house she finds her mother in the sun porch, watering the plants.

"Laurel wants me and Jill to be her mother's helpers," Phoebe says.

"That's Mrs. Murray to you," she answers.

"She said. She wants us to call her Laurel because she doesn't like being called Mrs. Murray. She says we would be there an hour a day."

"When did she ask you about this?" Phoebe's mother asks.

"Just now."

"I wish she'd spoken to me first."

"She is. Later," Phoebe says.

The sun porch is Phoebe's favourite room, even though it isn't even really a room. It has a big stuffed chair in it and a braided rug and plants that sprout violet petals.

Phoebe's mother sits down.

"You know, it's a good idea. But I'm a mother too, and I could use a helper like you."

Phoebe shuffles her feet. This isn't going to go her way, she can tell.

"Of course I'll have to pay you more than the allowance you get now, because your work load will go up," her mother adds.

"Well," Phoebe says, considering. "But then I won't see Jill."

"You'll be spending your whole summer with Jill," her mother says. "I'll tell you a secret. I want to spend an hour a day with my favourite daughter. How about that?"

"I'm your only daughter."

"Now, didn't I plan that well?"

"Oh, Mom," Phoebe curls her arms around her mother's neck. And rests there for a minute.

"Okay," she says. "But I won't make the brats' beds." She means her brothers.

———

Phoebe goes with Jill to Laurel's front door. She tells Laurel she can't come over because she already has a job as a mother's helper. Jill says yes to the job offer. "Don't bother talking to Bea," she adds. "She thinks it's a good idea." Jill never actually tells Bea about it, because she wants to keep all the ice cream money.

It is 4:26 when the girls leave.

Laurel moves to her front window, fussing baby on her hip. She feels like she is going crazy. Today, for no apparent reason, Kayla decided she hates peanut butter and will not eat it. Laurel put all the laundry in the machine and then realized she had no detergent. Laurel has downed three Aspirin and a pot of black coffee.

"No matter how bad it gets, one thing never changes," she mutters to a squirming Andrea. The Walker is in her yellow raincoat, even though there is not a cloud in the sky. Her head is down as she passes the house, exactly on time.

"That's it," Laurel says. And she's moving towards her front door, sliding her feet into a pair of flip-flops, taking her steps two at a time, rushing now so she can catch up to The Walker. The baby, happy to be outside with the warm glow on her skin, stops kicking. Laurel's strides are long and determined. She falls into step beside the raincoated figure.

"You are driving me crazy," Laurel says, angry.

The Walker says nothing, keeping her head down, her gaze focused a few feet ahead of her.

"I think you do this on purpose to drive me crazy," Laurel says.

Still no response.

"Okay." Laurel takes a deep breath. "Why are you going in circles like this?"

Silence.

Laurel reaches out, grabs her arm. The Walker flinches, stops, standing absolutely still on the street, head averted.

"Why are you doing this? Why are you going in circles?" Laurel demands again.

The Walker turns and looks directly at Laurel.

"Why are you?" she asks.

"I'm not," Laurel snaps angrily.

"Ah," she says. She pulls her arm free, carefully, and starts walking again. Laurel does not. She turns back towards her house, feeling suddenly deflated. She wants to sit in a dark room and cry, at least until her headache goes away, but now it's time to get the kids' dinner ready.

# CHAPTER 3

Bea wakes up suddenly and sits straight up in her bed, listening. The wine satin bedspread pools around her as she stretches to turn on the lamp. The hair on the back of her neck is bristling. She's listening hard but she can't make anything out. Something is wrong. She does not know what it is, but there is something wrong. The only time Bea wishes she were still married is late at night, when dread creeps in and she knows she is utterly alone. She learned the many nuances of dread in those months of turmoil and confusion getting out of Romania. Waking in the middle of the night, barely eighteen years old, Bea shivered like this under a thin blanket, holding her equally young husband, Peter. Scared, she would practise her school-girl English; please, she would say over and over in the darkness. Thank you, please. Peter would practise his German, believing then that they were destined to live in Berlin. But the Germans had other ideas, deporting the majority of fleeing Romanians as quickly as possible.

If Peter were here now he would laugh and stroll around the house turning on lights while she sank down into the covers. He was good at this. Now Bea has to get up and investigate alone, and she hates it.

She pulls on her robe and pushes her feet into her gold-threaded slippers. Bea crosses first to Delores' room where a small glow is cast by the night light. Delores is breathing deeply, everything is fine. Bea pulls the covers up over her, tucks her in more securely, smoothes her hair back from her forehead. For a moment her heart constricts as she stares at the small, perfectly rounded ear of her youngest daughter. Her baby girl, "my baby, mine," is how she thinks of Delores, totally different from Jill. Jill, who seems to belong to no one.

Bea continues down the hall to Jill's room, pauses outside the partially closed door. She cocks her head. She can hear something; it's faint, a clicking. She creeps into the room. Jill is asleep with her back to the wall, curled tightly into herself, like a fetus. Bea can see the steady rise and fall of her blankets. But the clicking is more distinct in here. It sounds like something is under the bed.

Bea gets down on her hands and knees beside Jill's bed, and puts her ear to the floor. A rustle, a sound like the material she works with all day sliding over the wooden work table. Her brow creases, she's puzzled. It must be coming from the basement.

Bea gets off her knees and heads down the hallway, turning on the kitchen light as she goes. She opens the door to the basement and quickly flicks on the stairway light. As soon as the light goes on she hears a sudden scurrying. There are creatures down there, alive and moving. She grips the banister, unable to move. A squirrel, she's telling herself, one squirrel must have found a way in. But she can hear rustling from different corners. There is more than one; it's a family of squirrels.

Bea puts a hand to her throat and the wildly beating pulse there. She can barely breathe. She cannot make herself go down those stairs into the basement. Leaving the light on, she quickly reaches for a kitchen chair and wedges it up under the doorknob. Bea backs away slowly, watching the door. She's shivering fiercely now, and she turns and runs down the hall. She climbs into her bed, into the circle of lamplight, arms hugging her knees to her chest. She catches sight of herself in the bureau mirror; white face, enormous eyes ringed by yesterday's eyeliner, tangled red hair glowing. Please, she says to herself softly. Please, please.

Jill is wide awake. She knew the instant her mother walked in her bedroom, because her body warned her. Jill listened hard, heard her mother turn around, go to the kitchen, then go back to bed. She made herself wait and count. She counted to one hundred, then one thousand. Bea must be asleep by now. Jill leans over her bed. The scurrying is directly underneath her. An urge stronger than fear is calling her to the basement.

Her fingertips tingle. She lifts the blanket, feet finding the cold hardwood floor. Barely breathing, Jill moves to her closet, creaking open the door an inch at a time.

She feels in the dark for the paper bag jammed at the back of her closet and pulls out two days' worth of black bread that she has not disposed of yet. She clutches it in her hand, and glides across the kitchen, a flickering shadow.

Jill finds the kitchen chair barricading the door to the basement. She tips it sideways, moves it. She opens the door and waits. She counts to ten. The click of nails on concrete comes to her; there is a flurry of rustles. Jill clutches the bread and descends one step at a time, down the top three stairs, to the landing. The dampness of the basement, the sticky coldness of it, oozes over her feet. She stares hard, her eyes adjusting to the dark, into the farthest corner of the basement where the rustling comes from.

There is a sudden stillness.

A large rat is pinned in the centre of Jill's stare.

Its eyes gleam at Jill, and there's a low, hissing sound. Jill does not move a muscle. Her heart is pounding, but she does not feel afraid. It feels the same as riding the roller coaster, a rush of wind, forcing her to breathe faster and harder, it is exhilaration.

Jill lifts her arm and throws the bread to the rat.

It moves quickly, snapping up the food, and Jill sees several smaller rats circling round, coming out of the dark. She can make out the shape of the work table and her mother's bolts of material strewn across the floor. The stairway light catches an arm and Jill strains forward, blinking hard. The mannequin is crooked. A rat's tail snakes around a plastic leg. Jill can see the other leg is chewed through, and the stump of Bea's mannequin is throwing everything off balance. The white face and vacant eyes give nothing away. To Jill, in the middle of the black night, huddled on the landing, this looks like a ghost lurching in the corner. She tilts her head, trying to make it stand straight again, but it will not.

Jill stands up slowly on her wooden legs, in a dream now, hovering. Jill can go either up or down, up to her room, or down to the scurrying world she has discovered lives beneath her bed.

Jill lifts her foot to a stair and finds she is going up, floating upwards.

Bea, sitting up in her bed, eyes wide open, hears the rustling, the door down the hall creaking shut, the give of Jill's mattress. The fear of the basement creatures enveloping her shifts to a new kind of starkness.

Bea is now afraid of her daughter.

———

Laurel wiggles into her bikini, and examines herself in her bedroom mirror. Her hips are generous, made for having babies. But as usual, she has gotten her figure back quickly. Not bad at all, for having given birth within the last year. She has lost the thirty pounds she put on during her pregnancy and the stretch marks are barely visible. Not bad at all. Laurel ties her hair up in a bouncy ponytail. It's an excellent day and the timing is perfect. Her two kids are at playgroup all morning. At noon Jill will be arriving and she will have help with the children for the rest of the afternoon. Right now, the baby is napping, and at 10:00 a.m. it is already hot and sunny outside. But most important, Laurel is happy because Gary is next door for two full weeks, building his loft.

Laurel checks on Andrea one last time, grabs the baby monitor, and heads out the door.

A ladder leans against the side of Gary's house. The sharp rap of a hammer comes from overhead.

"Hello," Laurel is calling as she starts climbing the ladder. Laurel is so intent on reaching Gary she does not notice that Janice, out watering her front rose garden, is watching her. Laurel's strong thighs and bare midriff ascend and disappear inside the gap at the roofline.

"Time for a break?" Laurel is calling as she climbs into the attic.

Gary stops swinging his hammer. He's wearing boots, jean shorts, and nothing else, the T-shirt he started out with this morning hanging from his back pocket. The grey hair on his chest is curling with sweat.

Shafts of sunlight and shadow stagger across the floor, giving the appearance of bars. Sawdust hangs off everything. Up here, it smells like sweat, and summer grass, and church pews.

Laurel breathes it in, steps forward, the bars of light playing across her flesh, across her face as she moves.

Gary knows exactly why she is here; they have been leading up to this for months. Gary knows this is wrong. It is stupid and risky and he loves Madeline. Laurel is using him. She is using him to prove that she is young and using him because she is angry, only her anger smells like seduction. This, Gary knows. But his hand reaches out for her anyway.

"This won't happen again," he tells Laurel. "Next time I'll keep you out."

"Shut up, Gary. You're the one who sent Madeline away. Don't try to hang this on me." And that is true. Gary did suddenly convince Madeline to take the boys, get away from the dust, and go to the lake for a week. He did that and he knows why. He was waiting for this.

Laurel and Gary are wrapped so tightly inside their cocoon of lies neither hears the faint creak of the ladder.

Jill is supposed to be reporting for duty at noon. She knows that. But Jill cannot wait to get to Laurel's house. Phoebe wanted her to go to Bird's Hill Park swimming with the other girls, because it is an in-service day off from school. Baby stuff, Jill thinks. She has a job now. This morning she dresses with special care, rummaging through her drawers until she finds her coolest black T-shirt with the pink "Girls Rule" slogan on the back. She checks the clock every fifteen minutes.

Jill decides there is no point in waiting until noon. Delores is mooching around the house getting on her nerves, and she could be taking Andrea for a walk now even if she does not get paid until noon. Jill grabs her key, slides it around her neck and heads down Glendale Avenue.

Her palms are sweaty as she starts up Laurel's driveway. Stops, because there is Laurel leaving the house, crossing the lawn. Jill thinks about calling out to her, telling her she is here early to play with Andrea, but she doesn't. Jill, with her ingrained spy instincts, instead ducks behind the hedge. Once Laurel is inside Gary's attic, Jill emerges and carefully, slowly, climbs.

Only the top of Jill's brown hair appears in the attic opening, blending into the dusty plywood floor. Jill's fingers dig into the cold metal rungs, and the cold is moving up her arms. She does not want to move and she does not want to look, because Laurel is doing something wrong. She is wrapped around Gary. Jill stares at her numbed elbows, stares so hard her arms are like a stranger's, they don't even seem to belong to her. Jill wonders, vaguely, why she does not slide bonelessly down the ladder since her arms are no longer there to hold her up. She wonders if this is how it feels to be a mannequin. Her thin arms are the same lily white. Jill knows these sounds, the grunting like Mr. Findley and Bea, knows exactly what is going on. Jill is very cold in the dark shadows. She won't look. She could, but she won't, because she is ashamed for Laurel and Gary is stupid for... Jill stops thinking. She can stop thinking when she wants to, just by breathing really deep. She breathes deeper. Now she can hear them talking.

"I don't like you, Gary," Laurel says loudly, feeling on the floor for her bikini bottoms and the baby monitor.

"No, Laurel," he says, leaning away. "You don't like yourself. I just got in the way."

He picks up his hammer, drops it. His shoulders slump. And now Gary does not like himself, and for the first time in two decades, he will not look directly into the eyes of his neighbours, his sons, or his wife.

Jill makes her legs move. She has to get out of here or she'll get caught. The blood rushes to her arms and hands and she is throbbing with painful pins and needles, but she keeps moving. Her foot finally feels ground and she crouches low and runs along Gary's hedge, arms dangling by her side, aching.

When Jill gets around to Laurel's side of the yard she goes directly to the baby carriage, standing empty near the back door. She kicks it, hard. The carriage bounces cheerfully. Jill heads to the river, and the rocks. Stupid job anyway, she's telling herself. She could go to The Nest and write about Gary and Laurel in the book. But Jill does not want to do that. She does not feel like a real spy at all. She just wants to sit by the rocks, where the river flows fastest.

Laurel backs out of the attic feet first, and inches down the ladder.

When she gets home, inside her house, she goes straight to the crib, seized by a sudden dread that the baby won't be breathing. But Andrea is fine, her tiny chest rising and falling, the skin so translucent Laurel can almost see her heart moving.

Laurel picks her up and nestles the baby into her breast reflexively. Laurel spends a long time in the rocking chair, nuzzling her baby's soft head.

—

Phoebe wakes up with one thought instantly bursting through her.

"It's my birthday. It's finally Friday, and I'm twelve like Jill!"

She hugs this to herself for a moment, then flings off her covers and bounds down the stairs. It is a sore spot for Phoebe that most of the year Jill is older than she is. Jill is practically thirteen, so it is about time she turned twelve.

"Yahoo," she yells into the kitchen, where her mother is sitting with her cup of coffee.

"Well, if it isn't the birthday girl," her mother says. "You definitely look older and wiser today. Happy birthday, honey." She gives Phoebe a quick kiss, and Phoebe is already skipping away. Her birthday is the most perfect day of the year, because it means it's practically summer holidays. School doesn't even count now, it's just report cards and field days and you don't have to learn anything new or do homework.

"Yum," Phoebe says, grabbing a juicy nectarine from the bowl of fruit in the middle of the table.

"And so what did you decide on for supper?" her mother asks. It's a tradition in this household that the birthday person can choose the menu, including a trip out for burgers.

Phoebe is ready. "Barbecued hot dogs and french fries and chocolate milk."

"And cake and ice cream?"

"Yup."

"And I take it you want Jill to eat over?"

"Yes, and sleep over. Mom..." Phoebe moves closer and twines an arm around her mother's neck. "...best mother in the whole world," she wheedles.

"What am I bracing myself for now?" her mother asks.

"Can Jill and I sleep outside in the tent? Please, please, please?" Phoebe holds her breath. This is a big treat, when her father sets up the nylon dome and blows up the air mattresses, and the tent is so far from the house in the back corner of the yard, it's like another universe where adults don't exist and anything can happen.

"Well, let me check the forecast and make sure there's no rain coming," her mother says.

"And if?" Phoebe pushes.

"If there's no rain, yes, you and Jill can sleep out in the tent."

"Yippee," Phoebe yells. "Thanks, Mom."

Last year on her birthday she did not sleep outside because they all went to a drive-in movie and conked out, Jill included, and had to be carried inside to bed at midnight. The year before, Jill had to go to her father's house on that weekend and missed Phoebe's birthday. Phoebe and her brothers tried sleeping in the tent but her brothers are such babies they got scared and as soon as it was dark they were blubbering and they all had to go back indoors.

This year would be different. This year she is practically a teenager.

The forecast calls for a half moon, clear skies, and a warm summer breeze. The school day drags by, even though it is mostly rehearsing for the end-of-the-year concert and making decorations for the gym.

Finally, Jill is arriving for supper and Phoebe's father is putting the tent up. They eat homemade chocolate cake with Oreo ice cream. Now the hardest part is waiting for dark.

"This is just like The Nest, isn't it?" Jill says as they crawl inside, armed with their comics and flashlights.

"Except better," Phoebe agrees.

"What do you mean?"

"'Cause we have a window and potato chips."

"And a whistle," Jill adds.

The whistle is to summon the adults. They have no intention of using it for real; they would rather die first.

"Maybe we should test it out," Jill says.

"That's a good idea," Phoebe says.

"You do it."

"No, you."

"Okay, pass it here."

Jill puts the whistle to her lips and blows so hard that Mr. Warbanski, five houses away, straightens from watering his tomato plants, believing for an instant that he is back at the rail yards and it is time to punch out.

Jill and Phoebe have collapsed in nervous giggles.

"Well, it works," Jill says.

Inside the kitchen, Phoebe's mother and father look at each other.

"Here we go," Phoebe's father says.

"You take the first turn," Phoebe's mother says.

"Should I scare them?" he asks, pushing his chair back, getting to his feet.

"Nah, not dark enough yet," Phoebe's mother says.

The girls are still laughing when Phoebe's father appears at their tent window.

"Ladies," he says. "Trouble here?"

"Just testing," Phoebe says. "The whistle works."

"That it does. I thought maybe it was a bear attack," he tacks on.

"Are there bears here?" Jill asks curiously.

"Oh no, I wouldn't think so," Phoebe's father says.

"But you don't know," Phoebe says.

"I don't know everything," he concedes. "Well, have fun. I must get in now, it's getting dark." And off he ambles, into the dusk.

Jill and Phoebe look at each other, wide-eyed, giggles returning at a higher pitch.

"This is fun," Jill says.

"Turn on the flashlight," Phoebe says.

"You should have come swimming yesterday. We had a gas. Tom and them were there, too," Phoebe says suddenly.

"Who cares about them anyway," Jill says.

Phoebe punches her in the arm, lightly.

"What did you do? I mean, in the morning."

Jill pauses. She's testing the words in her mind. Laurel was with Gary. I saw them. Then she pushes this away. She does not want it in the book. And for the first time, she does not even want to share these facts with Phoebe.

"So where were you?"

"I went to the Sev," Jill says nonchalantly.

"The 7-11? Just like that?" Phoebe is incredulous. The 7-11 is on the other side of the highway. Mostly teenagers from the high school hang out there. When Phoebe and Jill have to have Slurpees, they go together and wait and watch from across the road until there is no one hanging around outside.

"Were you scared?"

"Nah. Just some stupid boys there. No big deal."

Phoebe rolls onto her stomach, pondering this. It feels like a big deal to her. Maybe it will be easier to stroll through those boys like Jill now that she is twelve.

"Are you going to put it into the book?" Phoebe asks.

"Man, I wouldn't have even told you if I knew you were going to make such a big deal out of it," Jill says. Phoebe does not answer, but she feels a quick sense of hurt. Worse, she feels suddenly alone in the dark night.

"Do you know any good ghost stories?" Jill asks.

"No. I'm reading comics now." Phoebe turns away and grabs a comic book.

"Chicken."

"I am not."

"I know about an axe murderer," Jill presses.

Phoebe covers her ears, and Jill laughs.

"I don't really," she admits. "Pass me a comic."

They eat all the potato chips and read four comics each, lying on their stomachs, chins in their hand.

"Lasting longer than I thought," Janice says. She is standing in her darkened kitchen window, watching the glimmer of light wobbling in the tent. "It's almost eleven thirty."

"I think they'll make it this year," Gordon says.

"I'll just bring them something to drink, then," Janice says.

"I'm turning in," Gordon answers, giving his wife's arm a quick squeeze. "They'll whistle if they need us."

Janice picks her way across the black yard where her apple tree looms like a stranger. She's carrying lemonade and leftover cake. She can hear the murmur of voices from the tent.

"Girls," she calls, far enough away to give them time to adjust to her approach.

"It's just me. Coming in," she adds. A quick silence, then Phoebe is unzipping the tent's front flap.

"Mom?"

"Just me." And now she has arrived with her tray.

"Isn't it the middle of the night?" Phoebe asks, incredulous. By their figuring, it is now almost time for the sun to come up. Jill and Phoebe are quite sure they have stayed awake all night long, for the first time in their lives.

"Not quite," Janice says.

"Wow, thanks," Jill says, taking the cake and lemonade.

"We were starving to death," Phoebe adds.

"I'm going to bed now," Janice says. "Are you sure you want to stay out here all night?"

"Yes," Phoebe says quickly. "I'm twelve now, Mom."

"Yeah," Jill agrees. "I'll be thirteen in three months."

"Okay," Janice says. "Grab the flashlight and come use the bathroom one last time."

They trudge across the yard.

"Look up," Janice whispers.

"Oh," says Phoebe.

"Cool," says Jill.

The moon is a perfect half-pie against a sky studded with stars. It is so thick with stars, all shapes and sizes, it is almost glowing overhead.

When they step inside the hallway, still using the flashlight, it's the house that seems spooky and silent.

"This is weird," Phoebe whispers loudly, and her mother snaps on the hall light. The house shifts back into an ordinary place with ivy wallpaper and mint green walls. Phoebe blinks. But it still smells different in here in the middle of the night. There is something that changes for real when all the people she loves are away dreaming, and the TV and the computer are off and shadows up ahead are swallowing the kitchen. The house breathes deeper; it claims more for itself. It makes Phoebe shiver.

"Go wash up, girls," her mother says.

Jill and Phoebe brush their teeth together and even wash their faces, jostling and killing time, because now that they are inside it seems kind of stupid to go back across that long yard, to the tent so far away. When their eyes meet in the mirror and slide away, they know what the other is thinking, but they do not say it out loud.

"I'll watch you from the window," Janice says, when they finally get out of the bathroom.

Phoebe squares her shoulders. She takes Jill's hand as they step away from the house.

"It'll be okay," Jill says, low. "I'm not scared."

"Neither am I," Phoebe says.

Jill's eyes are sharp in the night, picking out a path clear of rocks and roots, steering them while Phoebe is still trying to adjust. It's Jill who knows the ground, who leads them directly to the tent, then flashes the light three times.

Phoebe is looking up again.

"What are you doing?" Jill demands.

"Let's lie out here for awhile," Phoebe answers. "Let's watch for shooting stars."

Jill shrugs, but Phoebe is determined. She's pulling the air mattresses out of the tent and positioning them just so, stretching out on her back.

"Turn off the light," she tells Jill.

Jill's stretches out beside Phoebe, the starry night pressing them down like a heavy quilt.

The sky is one shade bluer than black. Leopard frogs in nearby ditches fill the air with ribbit chants and the tips of trees rustle in a high up breeze. Down here, all is still.

"I see one," Jill says suddenly. "Look, it's a shooting star." She's pointing excitedly.

"I see, I see," Phoebe says, watching the point of light travel in a perfect arc over them. This is not a shooting star, Phoebe knows.

"It's a satellite," she announces.

"What?" Jill says, keeping her eyes glued to her discovery.

"See how it goes in a line so straight? My dad says those are cameras. There's lots of them up there."

"What are they taking pictures of?" Jill asks, skeptical.

"Us."

"I don't believe you."

"It's true. Some of them are taking pictures of us. Some are taking pictures of clouds and stuff, and some are spy cameras watching for bad things. That's what my dad says."

Jill is silent for a moment.

"Can they see us when we are in the bathroom and everything?"

Phoebe considers this new and awful possibility, which had not entered her mind before.

"I don't think they can go through the roofs of houses," she says.

"Good." Jill's voice echoes her relief.

They watch the satellite glide confidently between the stars.

"Should we wave?" Jill asks. "They must be watching us right now."

The girls wave.

Jill sits up and looks over at Phoebe.

"I just thought of something," she says. "Can the satellite see under the ground? To the rats under there?"

"Ugh," says Phoebe. "Stop it." She looks quickly to her left and right. She has become so absorbed in the light overhead she has forgotten for a minute how inky black everything is around them. Suddenly it seems quite possible a bear will come out of the bush in the backyard, looking for a meal.

"I'm just asking. Seriously," Jill says, lying back down.

"I think the ground stops them, like the roofs," Phoebe says.

"Too bad," Jill says.

"My dad says even the stars are not really real," Phoebe goes on.

"My daddy says, my daddy says," Jill mocks.

This is a sharp sting to Phoebe.

"I didn't say daddy, I said my dad. I'm not a baby." Phoebe is stiff now. She knows Jill is mad at her because Jill's father is not around much, and doesn't say anything to anyone when he is, not even Jill or Delores. She can't help it. It's not her fault Jill's father is so far away, even when he is close.

They lie quietly.

Slowly Jill moves her arm, so that her fingers find Phoebe's hand. Icy, like when Bea hits her. After a while she says, "How come the stars aren't real?"

They glint with so much whiteness now, merging into each other like daylight.

Phoebe is careful now not to say dad, daddy, father. "He says it takes so long for a star to shine its light down to us that by the time we see it, the star has already moved far, far away. The light up there right now means the real star is gone."

Jill is scrunching her nose.

"You mean that star, right there, is NOT there?" she points to the biggest one.

"Yeah. It is gone. Only the light stays behind for us, not the star."

Jill frowns.

"But you don't know that for sure," she says.

"I'm going to find out for sure," Phoebe says. "I'm going to be an astronaut."

"Yeah, right," Jill says.

"Am too," Phoebe insists. "I'm going to go up in a rocket and see the stars and mostly I'm going to follow those satellites and spy on them and put it in our book." She has figured this out completely just before falling asleep at night, but it's the first time she's said the words out loud, so she says them again, to hear how it sounds.

"I'm going to be an astronaut." Pause.

"Rockets blow up, Phoebe. It's a stupid idea."

"Shut up," Phoebe jabs her. "What are you going to be?"

"I don't know. A teacher maybe."

"Not still. Come on," Phoebe says. Since they were little they both said they would be teachers together and they planned to open their own school in the woods where children could play all day long.

"That was baby stuff," Phoebe says. "You have to be something when you grow up."

"I don't know, then."

"Wish on a star," Phoebe suggests. "That's what I did."

Jill studies the night. She wishes now for what she always wishes; that her father lived down the street here in Oakwood and that after school she could go to his house and cook supper because he always has food in his fridge. And he has books in his house that he loans her, interesting books about animals and Australia and Africa. Jill will never say this wish out loud, or trust it to the outside world of stars and birthday candles. It is a wish so deep inside her that only she can hear its soft whisper.

"Come on," Phoebe urges. "Think about what you will be when we grow up."

Jill tries tilting her head so she can see things both straight and crooked. She closes her eyes and squeezes them. She opens her eyes and blinks fast. Wishing as hard as she can, staring into her future in this fashion, Jill sees nothing. No picture of herself forms against the stars that are not really there.

"I don't know," she finally says again.

Phoebe feels a hint of panic, and squeezes her best friend's hand.

"You can be an astronaut with me," she says. "You can come on the rocket, too."

Jill tries this on, then shakes her head.

"I don't think so, Phoebe."

"We'll build a school house up there, then. Space children need teachers." She's trying hard now.

"Yeah, sure," Jill says, too easily. She slips her hand out of Phoebe's, tucking her arms under her head as a pillow, tired of the sky.

Phoebe stares up at the pinpricks of light so intently now her eyes blur. That star, there, is so close and so real, her father must have made a mistake. He's smart and everything, but he must be wrong about this. Phoebe sticks out her tongue, lying on her back in the yard on a June night, and her tongue touches the tip of the star. That is how Phoebe knows for sure it is real, because a star tastes like birthday cake.

Jill drags her air mattress back into the tent, and reluctantly, Phoebe follows with hers.

The girls make it through the night.

For some reason they cannot explain later, it is the milky stillness of dawn spilling into their tent that sends them running for the house, across the grass damp with dew, down into the rec room where they curl up like cats on the couch under the afghan.

———

"Here. If you walk her up and down the driveway in her carriage, she'll go to sleep," Laurel says, handing Jill the baby.

Andrea is fussing. She won't settle into her nap.

Jill is finally learning how to be a mother's helper.

She puts the baby gently into the carriage, holding her head the way Laurel showed her. She attaches the mosquito netting, then jiggles the carriage up and down. The crying quiets.

"Good," Laurel says. "Now just go back and forth on the driveway for a while, and she'll be out."

Jill walks, humming a little under her breath, saying baby words. Sometimes she tries to whistle because the baby tips her head and listens to the high notes, but she's not very good at holding it, so mostly she hums.

Jill has enough money to buy more than one ice cream now. Phoebe keeps bugging her, come on, let's go to the Dairy Queen, but Jill is not sure that's what she wants anymore. She likes holding the coins in her hands late at night; she likes rubbing the smooth surface and the ribbed edges. Ice cream melts so fast and then what will she have? So she's not sure anymore.

"I think she's asleep," Laurel calls. She is in the backyard, trying to dig past the weeds and stumps of old trees in the corner. She wants to plant a garden. Kayla and Jamie are playing in the grass, and trying to dig in the mud like their mother.

"She's asleep," Jill agrees, pushing the carriage over the grass, parking it under the oak tree.

"These weeds are impossible," Laurel says, sitting back on her heels, pushing her damp hair off her forehead. "I swear these dandelion roots go down about a mile. Come on," she says to Jill, standing up, brushing off her shorts.

Jill follows Laurel into the garage, blinking at the dimness.

"What, Mommy? Where you going?" Jamie is on his feet, following them.

"Just getting some stuff to kill the weeds," Laurel says dryly. "Don't panic."

"I want a Popsicle." Kayla is also in the garage now.

"Give us one minute here. Kayla, please go and watch the baby," Laurel says.

"I don't want to."

"Then no Popsicle."

Kayla turns reluctantly, goes back outside.

"Help me with this," Laurel says to Jill. She has the stepladder in her hands and the two of them drag it to the back of the garage.

"I need the Killex from up there," Laurel is explaining, pointing up at the shelf that runs the width of the garage six feet above the concrete floor.

"I'm a good climber," Jill offers.

"Yeah?" Laurel says. "Okay, up you go. I'll hold the ladder steady."

Jill climbs up the steps. She is studying the array of boxes and bottles and cartons neatly lined up on the shelf, reading the labels, eyes narrowed in the dusky light.

"The box we want should have a picture of a lawn mower on the front," Laurel says. "See it?"

"Okay," Jill says finally, reaching past several boxes for the weed killer. "Got it."

She climbs down the ladder.

"Thanks, Jill. I think that's it for today. It's just about time for me to start dinner. See you tomorrow?"

"Yes," Jill says. "Bye." But she walks over to the sleeping baby and rocks her for a while. She doesn't have to, but she likes the shade of the tree, the soft squeak of the carriage springs, and the chatter of Kayla and Jamie. She feels almost like she could fall asleep, too, it is so safe here.

# CHAPTER 4

Jill asks, "Do you think we should we put it in the book?"

"What?" says Phoebe.

"The rats. Should we put it in the book how we got them to come to my house?" Jill says.

"I don't know." Phoebe has to think about this. They are riding their bicycles towards the graveyard. Everything they've written about in the spy book so far has happened when they are together. But the rats belong to Jill. Jill discovered them and Phoebe has never even seen them. This is the first time they have had to face the possibility of separate lives. It makes Phoebe feel cheated.

"I don't think we can write it in," Phoebe says finally.

"I think we should," Jill insists. "I saw them."

"Maybe if we both see them together?" Phoebe says.

Jill maneuvers her bike around a pothole, pedaling towards their spot.

"I heard Bea on the phone this morning," Jill says. "Some men are coming tonight to search for the rats. Can you come over?"

"Okay, I'll try. Then we'll see them together and we can put it in the book," Phoebe agrees. The crows are cawing loudly, swirling overhead in the lengthening afternoon shadows.

"Are they going to catch them?"

"I dunno," Jill says. "I guess maybe."

Jill has noticed something as they ride.

"Look," she says, pointing to the newer area of the graveyard. "New hole."

Phoebe turns to the right, and they pedal quickly. The smell of freshly dug earth makes her think of apples.

Jill and Phoebe toss aside their bikes and walk closer, skirting the pile of earth. The hole, just bigger than a coffin, has been crisscrossed with planks of wood as a temporary guard.

Phoebe peers down through the planks.

"No one in there yet. Must be for tomorrow," she says. The girls know the graveyard routine. In the special section of their book called Ghosts and Spirits, they will record the digging of this plot and the name of who gets buried here once the headstone goes up. Sometimes it takes months for the headstone to be erected, but that's okay. They fill in the details later.

Jill is squatting by the edge of the hole, peering down. She's frowning.

"Are there rats down there?" she asks finally. They've never seen any in the graveyard.

"Maybe," says Phoebe. This thought gives her the creeps; she takes a step back.

"There must be. That's where they come from, down there," Jill says. She sits back on her heels, thinking.

"Whatever," Phoebe says. "Let's go to our spot now." She's already turning away, towards the bikes.

"Wait." Jill cannot move. She's trying to grasp this. "Phoebe, there's a whole world down there." She jumps up. She looks down at the ground with new eyes, squinting, making things crooked. This is what the mannequin was trying to tell her in the middle of the night. She is sure of it.

"Look," she says to Phoebe. She's pointing down. She's getting excited, and squeaky. "There are rats and other things right under us right now, right under our street and our house, waiting to come up. Do you see?"

Phoebe feels prickly. She does not like this one bit.

"I don't think there's that much down there," she says. "Anyway, look up." She points to the sky. "There are birds and clouds and angels up there. So." This makes things even for Phoebe.

"It's different," Jill says stubbornly.

"No, it's not."

Jill sits down hard, and covers her ears. She's trying to press what she knows into her brain, the enormity of the unseen slithery things moving beneath her in the blackness of night, looking for ways to surface. She's tuned Phoebe out.

"...fine, I'll see you later." Phoebe is on her bicycle now, poking Jill with the front wheel.

"What?" Jill is scrambling up.

"I'm going home to do my homework, so that maybe my mother will let me come over after supper. If I don't get it done I'll never be allowed," Phoebe says. She has seized on this as a good reason to leave, but really she wants to get away from Jill and the open grave.

"Okay," Jill says. She sits by the hole. She wants to see what will move down there, if she is quiet. After Phoebe leaves and the crows start screeching and swooping, the breeze feels chilly, giving her goosebumps. Jill stays ten minutes, and then she is on her bike, too, racing for the wrought iron gate.

—

"No," Phoebe's mother says firmly, passing around second helpings of mashed potatoes and corn niblets.

"But, Mom, I've done all my homework. And it's practically summer holidays."

"It's a school night," her mother insists.

"Well, there goes my only chance to ever see a rat." Phoebe has decided to share this information. She's not sure why, but she wants her mother to know not everything is as it seems at Jill's house.

"Can you explain that?" her mother asks. Jill's two younger brothers are squirming at the dinner table. Her father is still at work. At the mention of rats, Brad and Gordie stop yanking and poking at each other to listen.

"Jill saw them. Big fat rats in her basement. They were there last night."

"Really." Her mother sits back. The girls aren't making this up, she knows. It rings true.

"And some men are coming after supper to get them. Now do you see why I need to go to Jill's?"

"Well, I'm afraid the answer is still no. Rats carry diseases, you know. It's no place for kids. We'll just let the men do their work in peace."

"But, Mom."

"No buts. Where are the rats coming from? Did she say?"

"Under the ground. That's what Jill says."

"But how are they getting into the basement, and why?" Phoebe's mother presses.

Phoebe shrugs. "I don't know." She has to speak loudly, because her brothers have now started a chorus of "we wanna see the rats, too." Gordie is hammering a spoon on the table at the same time.

"What if Jill needs me?" she says to her mother.

"Why would she need you?" she asks, head tilted sideways. She pauses with the bowl of potatoes in her hand, watching Phoebe's face.

"I don't know." Another shrug. "Sometimes she just does." Phoebe has a queasy feeling about Jill being in the house with Bea and the rats, alone. For five years Phoebe has clutched Jill's cold hand. Phoebe avoids her mother's eyes, pushes her chair back from the table.

"I don't want any more. May I be excused?" she asks.

"Yes."

"Rat girls," Brad says gleefully and flings a corn niblet at her back.

Phoebe turns, hands on her hips. "Don't make me hurt you," she says with the confidence of someone three years older and thirty pounds heavier than her as-yet-undeveloped nine-year-old brother.

"As if," Brad snorts, but he turns to bug his younger brother instead.

—

Jill is home with Delores watching TV when her mother comes in from work. Delores jumps up and turns off the TV because it gives Bea a headache.

"Hi, Mom. Bea," she says.

"Hi. Here." She hands Delores a grocery bag.

Jill does not say anything, making herself invisible on the couch, until she sees the high-heeled shoes slipped off, the toes wiggling and the hand sliding the black leather away, into the closet. Jill studies each tiny motion. Safe.

"Hi, Bea," she says then.

"Hi. How was school?" Bea asks.

"Good." Jill gets up off the couch and moves towards the kitchen to set the table. There will be a real supper tonight, with boiled potatoes and carrots and thick salami slices. Jill allows her hunger to surface, allows her stomach to growl.

"Put those potatoes on to boil, Delores," Bea is calling over her shoulder, heading to her bedroom to change. "We have company coming in one hour."

Jill does not ask if it's the rat men. She and her mother have not discussed the rats in the basement.

Bea's mother dresses with care, and redoes her make-up just in case one of the visitors is single. She applies perfume while Delores and Jill prepare supper, get everything on the table.

"Ready," Delores says, going to her mother's room. "You look pretty."

"Thank you." Bea twirls in front of the mirror. "So do you. Want some rouge?"

"Yes." Delores bounces onto the bed next to her mother, closes her eyes to savour the soft brush against her skin, the smell of her mother so near, leaning over her.

"There you go," Bea says.

Delores sees her pink cheeks in the mirror. Bea gives her a quick kiss, leaving behind a faint outline of lipstick. Delores will not rub it off; it's hers now.

———

Phoebe's mother is moving quietly through her kitchen, preparing a second dinner for her husband, who's arrived home late from work.

Phoebe and her brothers are supposed to be asleep by now. But Phoebe often lies awake later than she is supposed to, listening to the hum of the fridge or in winter, the furnace, the flow of the television, an ambulance siren moving somewhere in the distance, in another neighbourhood.

Tonight it's the soft murmur of her parents' voices she hears. Usually this lulls her to sleep like rain tapping on the roof, but sometimes she strains to hear what they are talking about, which she can do if she breathes hardly at all, and lies perfectly still.

"...Jill and Delores. I just don't like it," her mother is saying.

"Have any of the other neighbours mentioned a rat problem this year?" her father asks, tucking into his steak.

"No. That's just it."

Phoebe can hear the scrape of a fork and knife against a plate.

"I'm not sure," her mother goes on. "They've been friends for so long, what?, five or six years now..."

"But?" says her father.

"Well," says her mother, "I think that woman Bea is anorexic, she is so thin. I don't know, I've tried making friends with her, but she is so... What word am I looking for?" There is a long pause. A branch taps lightly against Phoebe's bedroom window.

Phoebe can almost hear her father shrug, the way he does when he does not agree with her mother but does not want to start a fight. Her father does not gossip. "I'm sure it hasn't been easy for her," he says finally.

Her mother is quiet a moment.

"But do you ever watch the way Jill eats when she is here? Like she can't get it in fast enough. Both she and Delores are barely making it through school. And now the rats. I just don't like Phoebe going over there."

Phoebe hears a spoon clinking against a mug, stirring what she knows is her mother's nightly cup of tea. She's afraid to hear what's next. If she can't play with Jill, she'll die. Or they will have to run away. That could be fun, now that she thinks of it. They could stow away on a plane, maybe.

"Well, maybe we should have them over here more often," her father says. Phoebe breathes a sigh of relief.

"Jill is helping Laurel Murray this summer a few hours a day. Like a mother's helper."

"There you go," says her dad. He gets up to take his dishes to the sink. "They won't have time to get into trouble over at that house."

"I guess," her mom says. But her voice still holds some doubt, and Phoebe knows she'll have to be extra careful.

Last year, Phoebe almost spilled the beans about stuff at Jill's house. "I'm telling my mother that your mother hits you," Phoebe had announced. Jill had a parade of bruises marching from her knee to her hip that time.

"No," Jill said, and her voice was high and panicky.

"My mom will stop it," Phoebe said.

"No, she won't. The social workers will come, stupid." Jill was plucking at the grass, pulling it up with quick, jerky motions.

"What social workers?"

"When I was in Grade Two, the teacher asked me and I told, and the social workers came." Jill was talking fast, needing to impress on Phoebe why silence was so important.

Phoebe looked puzzled.

"I don't remember this," she said.

"I never told you."

This is almost beyond comprehension to Phoebe. They told each other everything. Didn't they?

"What?" Phoebe said.

"It was stupid," Jill said. They were inside The Nest, and Jill crawled out and started pacing, and fidgeting with her hair, twirling it round and round.

"I still don't get it." Phoebe frowned.

"Two social workers took me to the principal's office and they wanted me to say how bad Bea is and how she hits me and everything."

"Well, she does," Phoebe said.

"No. She doesn't mean it." Jill turned to Phoebe, fierce and angry, fist clenched. "She told me she doesn't mean it. Take it back." Her body dared Phoebe to say something, because she wanted to fight with her.

"Yeah," Phoebe said. "Anyways."

The rigidity went out of Jill's body.

"The stupid social workers will take us to my father's, for good. That's what Bea told me. That's what will happen," Jill said, her voice low.

A picture of Jill's father pops into Phoebe's head. He whistles all the time. Jill and Delores sleep at his place one weekend every month, and Phoebe has been there once for a sleepover, too. It was okay. There were lots of potato chips in his house, but he lives so far away. It takes an hour to go there in the car and even calling there on the phone is long distance.

If Jill had to move there, it would be a disaster for Phoebe.

"That would be the worst," Phoebe said.

Jill looked up. "No, it wouldn't," she said. "He's okay." And then she punched Phoebe in the arm, hard.

"Cut it out." Phoebe rubbed her shoulder and was surprised to realize for the first time that Jill liked her father. Maybe Jill even wanted to move away.

"But I don't want to go to a different school and everything," Jill added quickly, as though reading Phoebe's thoughts.

"You can't," Phoebe agreed. That was that.

"So you have to promise you won't say anything. Not to your mom or anyone," she said to Phoebe.

"I won't," Phoebe promised, because she could not bear the idea of her best friend being sent away, where they would hardly ever see each other again.

"Blood swear," Jill pressed.

Phoebe's eyes lit up. They had not done this for a while, blood sisters. Riding home, getting a knife from the kitchen, pricking the tip of a finger, smearing their blood together, kisses on the lips. It was a ceremony for big occasions that always made them feel better, and this was one of those times.

Now Phoebe is lying in her bed. It was probably dumb to have told about the rats. She hopes she hasn't gotten Jill into trouble.

———

The two men are big and even though their business is poison, they are cheerful.

"Are you sure it was rats you saw?" one of them is saying to Bea as he moves through the front hallway and kitchen to the basement door, assessing the tidy bungalow. No garbage or empty beer bottles or food scraps left out, he notes to himself as he moves. "Most likely mice. That's what we usually see in basements." He doesn't say that in the middle of the night, people have a way of seeing creatures ten times bigger than life. He's used to this.

"It is rats," Bea says flatly. She is remembering the dark basement apartment where she had waited with the other refugees, waited and waited for the courier to come, to take them across the border in the middle of the night, to safety on the other side. She had burrowed into Peter, sick much of the time in the early stages of pregnancy although she did not realize that right away. She remembers sickness and dread, the sound of rats, the feel of their presence. Scurrying rats in dark corners, chewing. Rats are always in corners chewing, she knows. She never saw them then and she does not have to see them now. Her body remembers.

The exterminator is reaching for the basement door. Bea visibly straightens, shaking off her fear. He keeps a straight face as he moves the kitchen chair away.

"Well, me and my partner will go down and see. Is this the light switch?"

"Yes," Bea says clearly. "And there is another light at the bottom of the stairs."

Their boots are heavy on the stairs.

Jill slips past her mother, blending into the shadow of these big men, following them down.

Delores and Bea stay in the kitchen.

"Cripes," the man says, under his breath. "It had to be rats that did this."

Bolts of material are unfurled and shredded on the basement floor. The mannequin stares blankly at them, one leg and an arm amputated. It is cold in the basement. Jill sits on the bottom stair, keeping her feet off the basement floor, just in case.

"Rat droppings," the second man says, walking to the darkest corner.

"The sewer?" the first one guesses.

"I'll go get the stuff," says the second one, and he clomps past Jill and back up the stairs, out of the house to the truck.

"Did you see them?" the first man asks Jill.

"No," she lies.

"Well, here's the problem." He's swinging his heavy flashlight to the sewer grate in the middle of the basement floor. The second worker has returned, with a box, traps, a long metal rod with a hook.

"Don't know why the grate is off this hole, but that's how they're getting in here," the first one says. Jill curls into herself, trying to become invisible. Realization hits her like a bolt. She and Phoebe forgot to put the grate back on the sewer. They forgot.

The man shines his light down the sewer.

"Looks like some blockage," the second one says, leaning over him. He's fishing with the long rod. He grunts as he gives it a yank.

The first man walks to the bottom of the stairs, where Jill is hugging her knees to her chest.

"Mrs..." he calls upstairs, then pauses.

"Call me Bea," she says, appearing at the top of the stairs.

"We found the problem. I think you should come down here."

"Do I have to?" she asks.

"It would be best," he answers.

Bea descends in her spike-heeled shoes. She clutches the railing when she sees her limp mannequin, leaning heavily against the wall.

"I don't want to see this," she says.

"We can fix it," the man says.

Bea wobbles across the concrete. Jill can't help staring. She has never seen her mother wobble, she has never seen her weak, not ever. Bea puts her hand on the man's arm, leaning into him.

He pats her hand reassuringly.

"This is why they're coming," the other man says, and he pulls up the metal rod, with the soggy bread hooked on the end. "I think there are loaves of this down the sewer."

"And with the grate off," the first man adds, "this has become a food base for them. And an easy, dry place to spend the night."

Jill's face is burning hot. She doubts she could run, even though that's what she wants to do. She tries to stand up.

Bea looks over at her.

"Stay where you are," she says.

Jill sits.

"What will you do now?" Bea is calm again.

"I'm going to have to unplug this line, fish out all the bread," the first man says.

"Then we'll use poison. We pour it down the hole. It kills them pretty fast."

"I don't want dead rats in my basement," Bea says.

"No, I doubt any will make it this far," the man says. "But we'll bait a few traps and come back in a few days. The main thing is to keep the grate on and the sewer clean. Any idea what was happening down here?" he adds.

"Jill?" Bea says, without looking over at her.

Jill is too strangled to speak. She's watching the second man pour the white powder from the silver box into a container of gruel.

"I mix it with food, so they don't know what's hit them until it's too late," he tells Bea.

"I want to thank you gentleman for your help," Bea says, striding back to the stairs. "It's your bedtime, Jill," she says when she passes her daughter.

Jill follows her mother upstairs, and goes into her room. She closes the bedroom door, but she sits up in her clothes in the dark, waiting.

When Jill hears the front door open, the thank yous and good byes, the slam of the truck door in the driveway, she braces herself. Her bedroom door swings open, and the light from the hallway spills around her mother so that she looks exactly like the mannequin downstairs. White, flat, without features.

"You did this," the mouth snaps at Jill. The teeth shine. "You made those rats come."

"Yes," Jill says clearly. She stands up, and starts walking towards Bea.

"I should have taken the money when I had the chance," Bea says. Jill stops, cocks her head, watching Bea's face crumple. Bea rubs her eyes. It would have been so easy then, Bea's thinking. North American couples had flocked overseas when the Ceausescu regime toppled, offering thousands of American dollars to eighteen-year-old Romanian girls with healthy infants. Her value went up substantially; she was no longer a poor, gypsy refugee, and all through her pregnancy Bea thought about the money, thought about going to live in California, studying design at college. She thought about the growing thing in her stomach as a commodity. It was Peter who said no. Nineteen-year-old Peter promised they would make a new life in Canada and keep the baby, his great-aunt and uncle offered to sponsor them to come live in Winnipeg. His uncle could get him a job at Siemens. Finally, Bea had agreed. Jill was born two months after they arrived.

Now Jill takes another step forward.

"I can do it again. Anytime I want," Jill says. "I can make the rats come back." The sound is so strong and low in her throat it's a new voice.

"Don't," Bea says. "Stop it."

Something has shifted so completely, Jill feels she could fly, or move a mountain. What is coursing through her veins is like thick, sweet chocolate syrup. Her eyes, glinting in the darkened room, look exactly like the eyes that spear through the blackened basement. Bea takes another step back.

"I won't eat that bread," Jill says.

Bea is moving down the hallway. She shuts her bedroom door behind her, and takes the chair from the vanity and wedges it under the handle.

She will never hit Jill again.

Jill will never crouch, cornered, again.

The next day there is no black bread with margarine in Jill's lunch box. There is nothing at all.

———

Gary is still on holidays, but every time Laurel looks over the fence, he has one of his sons helping him, carrying boards up the ladder, hammering and sawing. Laurel offers them lemonade sometimes, which the boys drink in big gulps and which Gary refuses. He drinks water out of the hose, the cold water running down his chest.

But today, Gary is alone.

He has the leash out and Cody is barking and running in circles. Gary is taking the dog for a walk.

Laurel is seeing this from her kitchen window. She gets Andrea into her stroller.

"Kayla, Jamie, we're going to the beach. Hurry up, grab your pails."

They come scrambling up the stairs from the basement playroom. Kayla finds the pails but no shovels. Laurel gives them soup spoons from the kitchen, anxious to get moving.

By the time Laurel settles herself near the swings, Gary is at the far end of the beach. That's good. He hasn't noticed them arrive; it does not look like she's chasing him.

He's walking back towards them, squinting out over the river, the dog trotting at his side.

"Hi, Gary! Hi, Cody," Kayla yells and takes off running. Jamie is too absorbed vrooming his truck in the sandbox to bother.

"Hi there. Having fun?" Gary says, his gaze moving past Kayla, finding Laurel pushing the baby in a swing. Kayla pats the big dog's head. He stands still for her, as he always does.

"I'm making chocolate cakes." Kayla announces. "Come see."

She drags Gary to the sandbox, to inspect her upside-down sand pies, which she is decorating with rocks.

"Can I eat one?" Gary asks.

"No, silly." Kayla giggles.

"Well, you let me know when they are ready. I'm just going to talk to your mom."

"No. She's my mom," says Jamie.

"Okay, I'm going to talk to your mom, too."

"Me, too." Jamie is on his feet, following Gary.

Gary walks over to Laurel, who is at the bench now with Andrea on her lap.

"Are you avoiding me?" Laurel asks, smiling over at him.

"Yeah," he sighs. "I am."

"I have a mother's helper now. Jill. I can get away for an hour." She reaches down and prods Jamie towards the swings.

"Don't want to," Jamie whines.

"Then here, " Laurel says handing him a spoon. "Go collect sand for me, honey."

This appeals to Jamie, who starts back towards the sandbox where Kayla is still making pies.

"Yeah, I've seen Jill hanging around," Gary picks up the conversation. "I don't think it's a good idea, Laurel."

"There's no reason why we can't be adult about this," Laurel says. Her tone is light and breezy, she's saying "live a little, you deserve it," and that easy smile is there.

Gary forces himself to look away, because he's already leaning towards the invitation.

"I'm not sure what it is you're looking for, Laurel, but it's not me," he says finally.

"I'm looking for sex, Gary. That a problem for you?" She's slightly mocking now.

He laughs out loud, looks at her straight again.

"Good try, Laurel. Come on, Cody. Time for us to go home." Gary reaches down and scratches his dog behind the ears, then he turns on his heel and leaves. Laurel stares down at Jamie and the few grains of sand he has carried to her so carefully in his spoon.

—

Janice is enjoying the sun on the back of her neck as she hoses down her garden when Laurel comes up her driveway, with the baby stroller and the two little ones.

"Nice day," Laurel says. "Do you have time for tea?"

Janice hesitates. Laurel sees it. And yesterday, she had walked down the street to visit, something she used to do easily enough, and Janice had made up excuses about scrubbing the basement, too busy to stop. Laurel knew they were excuses because Janice looked past Laurel when she talked, not meeting her eyes, not like Janice at all.

"Okay," Janice says, and leans over to turn off the water.

"Out back, in the sun?" Laurel asks, herding Jamie and Kayla to the backyard, pushing the stroller, settling herself at the picnic table.

Janice fetches cups, spoons, juice, and cookies. They chat about anthills in the grass, and the summer sale at The Bay.

"Come to my house for coffee tomorrow," Laurel is saying, but Janice is already shaking her head.

"What?" Laurel presses.

Janice puts down her spoon, looks Laurel in the eye.

"I've known Madeline a long time," she says. "A lot of years. Her sons were just little when we moved in here. She used to watch Phoebe for me when she was a baby, when I needed to run to the store. That's all I'm saying."

Laurel stands up.

"Fine," she says.

There's a clatter on the driveway as Jill and Phoebe come barreling into the backyard on their bikes.

"Cookies," Phoebe says, diving for a fistful, passing half to Jill.

"Hi, Jill, Phoebe," says Laurel, as Kayla and Jamie swarm to the bikes, already pressing Jill's leg and taking ownership of her. Jill is awkwardly pleased by the easy affection.

"Where have you been?" Phoebe's mother asks.

"Oh, around," Phoebe says.

Laurel is moving her children down the driveway, almost sauntering as she waves an airy goodbye, as though she does not have a care in the world. Janice watches her go, then briskly turns her attention to the girls.

"What are you two doing at that graveyard all the time?" she asks.

Phoebe and Jill look at each other quickly, chewing hard.

"What do you mean?" Phoebe says.

"I ran into Mrs. Gustafson in the store," her mother says. The Gustafsons live at the edge of the graveyard. "She says you two are always in there, poking around and disappearing. What's up?"

"Nothing," Phoebe says. "We're just playing."

"Right," her mother says. But now she needs to know, so when Jill and Phoebe get back on their bikes, heading down the street, she follows them, walking leisurely, waving to the Warbanskis.

"How is Joey?" she calls to them. "Haven't seen him in a while." She had gone to school with their son Joey; he was one grade ahead of her. She hadn't lived in this house on Glendale Avenue then, the way Joey did. She grew up on the other side of the boulevard, in the apartments.

"He's fine," Mrs. Warbanski says. "Thank you for asking."

"Say hello to him for me," she says.

"We will."

When Janice gets inside the cemetery she moves quickly, positioning herself behind an oak tree, in the shadows. The girls' bikes are lying on the ground about twenty feet away. They're in here somewhere. This may take awhile. Janice traces the ridged bark with her finger, smiling at the way the swirls play with the sunlight filtering through the leaves. She feels herself relaxing. It's so calm she can hear the bees buzzing and the grasshoppers clicking their legs. No wonder the girls like it in here.

Janice waits, and sure enough, Phoebe and Jill crawl out from under a bush, circle around and pull their bicycles into view, and then they are off.

She cannot believe she is thirty-nine years old, down on her hands and knees in a graveyard trying to squeeze herself through a hole that's too small in some bushes. No one told her this is what she signed on for when she had kids.

"Oh," she says out loud, when she gets inside. "It is perfect."

She's sitting cross-legged. There's just enough room for one adult, or two girls.

"There's that old blanket," she says, reaching out to stroke the nubs on the grey quilt that disappeared from her rec room last summer. She breathes in deep and the musty smell brings a quick spurt of recognition. She can see herself and her sister in their fort. They have draped an assortment of old curtains and blankets over the picnic table in back of the apartment complex. It's one of those endless summers and they crawl into their fort every single day and play Barbies. At this moment it feels like yesterday. It could not have been thirty years ago; she can clearly see Barbie's bald spot where they had to cut her hair off because of the bubble gum that got all tangled in her tresses.

Janice leafs through the stack of comics. At the bottom of the pile, she finds the notebook. She pulls it out.

JILL AND PHOEBE. BLOOD SISTERS, it says on the cover, in black magic marker. PRIVATE. TOP SECRET. KEEP OUT. THAT MEANS YOU!!!!

Janice laughs out loud, and she is so tempted to open the book and read all the top secrets that her fingers itch. But she does not. She puts it back carefully, under the pile of comics, exactly as she found it.

At the corner of the blanket she finds two cigarettes and matches.

"I don't think so, gals," she says. And these she does slip into her pocket. With one last look around, Janice crawls out of her girlhood summer, crawls over her high school graduation, a marriage, the birth of three children. She crawls out of The Nest. She wishes she didn't have to.

# CHAPTER 5

**B**rian is flipping hamburgers on the grill, enjoying a nice, cold beer on a warm summer evening. Laurel has just come back from the store with the buns and can finally put her feet up. The baby is fed, and the other two are happy to slurp chocolate milk and eat picnic-style on a blanket in the grass. It's better than sitting up straight at the table.

"What is that?" Brian says, frowning.

"I know," Laurel says. "I was wondering the same thing. It's like a whimpering or something." They both double-check, but all three kids are settled.

"Well, not ours," she says, sliding lower into her chair.

"I think it's coming from Gary and Madeline's," Brian says.

"None of our business," Laurel says quickly.

But Brian is getting to his feet, putting his beer bottle down.

"Maybe they want privacy, Brian, ever think of that?" Laurel says. She does not want him going over there, poking into things.

"I'll be discreet," Brian says, and there is no stopping him. He's walking towards the fence.

"Definitely coming from the other side of their house," he says over his shoulder. He walks around, opens the gate to Gary and Madeline's yard, goes through it. Laurel is tensing; she rubs the back of her neck.

"Where's Daddy?" Kayla asks.

"Next door. He'll be back in a sec."

And Brian is walking back quickly, motioning to Laurel. His face is tight.

"What?" Laurel is on her feet.

"Get the kids in the house. Something is wrong with Cody. It looks like rabies or something. He's down and whimpering over there," Brian says.

"Is that all?" Laurel says.

"Is that all?" Brian snaps. "I'm going to find Gary."

"Wait, I just meant..." She falters.

"I don't think the kids should be out here." Brian is already striding back to Gary's house, banging on the side door.

Laurel is turning off the gas barbecue, moving the kids. They want to stay outside. "Picnic," Jamie says, over and over, sitting heavy and square, refusing to stand up, digging his heels into the grass.

Gary is coming to the side door, propping it open with his foot, coffee mug in hand, glancing past Brian to Laurel, then back to Brian. He's frowning at whatever Brian is saying. They're moving out of sight, going around the side of the house.

Laurel is trying to make Jamie stand up. Stubbornly, he keeps his knees bent.

"Kayla, if you get inside right now, you can watch *The Lion King*." Laurel is ready to divide and conquer, and use bribes. Kayla sprints for the door, whooping. It works. Jamie can suddenly stand just fine and follows Kayla downstairs. Laurel puts Andrea next to them in her playpen with an uncooked hot dog.

She pops the movie into the VCR then goes back upstairs to the back door, craning her neck.

She sees Gary dragging the dog. There is a howling now that reaches through the open windows and into several houses on Glendale Avenue. It's a howl that hurts the ear, and makes the hair on the back of a neck bristle. It's a howl of death. Laurel moves, closing windows. She stands in the kitchen covering her ears. She can still hear the howling. She goes into the basement and watches the movie with the kids, cranking up the volume.

She's at the kitchen table when Brian comes in, three hours later. He goes directly to the sink, scrubs his hands and forearms, sits down heavily at the table.

Laurel covers his hand with her own.

"Cody died on the way to the vet's. He says it doesn't look like rabies, it's more like poisoning." Brian looks up.

"What kind of poisoning?" Laurel asks.

"The vet says another dog has already been brought in tonight from this neighbourhood. He thinks something is going on."

"What do you mean?"

"He's doing autopsies. He thinks it's possible the dogs were deliberately poisoned."

"I don't believe that," Laurel says.

"I know. It gives me the creeps." They sit in silence for a minute.

"How is Gary?" she asks.

"He's holding up, but Madeline is a mess. She says she picked Cody. He was the runt of the litter, but he grew up to be the most handsome. That's what she kept saying. Both of their boys are out tonight, so they don't know yet."

"Well," she says, studying their linked fingers.

"Yeah," says Brian, and he sounds exhausted.

———

Jill turns off the TV. Bea is late. It is almost dark out. Jill slides across the shiny kitchen floor in her sock feet. Bea waxed it this past weekend. Delores comes into the hallway.

"What are you doing?" she asks.

"Steal anything good lately?" Jill asks breezily.

"Shut up," Delores says.

"I'm just kidding," Jill says. "I have a good idea. I need your help. Okay?"

"Okay. What?"

"Come with me." She grabs her sister's hand and heads to the basement door. Delores is pulling back, trying to skid to a stop.

"I don't want to go down there," she says plaintively.

"There's nothing down there," Jill says.

"Yes, there is. You're lying."

"Listen, the men made them go away."

"I still hear them," Delores says.

"I'll check first. Okay, baby?" Jill lets Delores' hand go and opens the basement door. She walks down the stairs to the first landing.

"See? Nothing," she calls back up.

"I don't want to, Jill."

"Fine. I don't care," Jill answers, and she turns on the basement light, continues down the stairs to the cold cement floor. Nothing. She knows that the rats are safe, running under the streets of Oakwood, for now.

Jill makes her way directly to the mannequin propped in its corner. She grasps it by its one good arm, and drags it across the basement floor, thump, thump, thump up the stairs.

Delores, almost eight years old, is standing in the kitchen sucking her thumb.

When Delores sees the white leg coming through the door into the kitchen she hits it, as hard as she can.

"Stop it, Delores. This is heavy." Jill is struggling under the weight of the mannequin, moving it slowly into full view.

"I don't want it," Delores is saying. "Take it away, Jill."

"I'm doing Bea a favour," Jill says.

"You're going to be in trouble."

"Big deal," Jill says. She lets the mannequin slide to the floor and sits down in a chair to catch her breath after the climb up the stairs with her load.

"What are you doing with it?" Delores asks, and now she's circling closer to the torso, prodding it with her toe.

"Bea doesn't go down there to sew anymore," Jill says, "so I thought I'd bring this to her." She grins. "See, it's a favour."

Delores still looks skeptical.

"Grab the foot," Jill tells her sister. "I need help carrying it."

Jill is on her feet again, lifting the mannequin by its armpits, and now Delores does help. She takes hold of the leg.

"Okay, I'm going to back down the hall. We're taking it to Bea's room."

"She won't like that," Delores says.

Jill does not bother answering.

She stands the white body on its one good leg in the corner, at the end of the dresser. Jill reaches for Bea's cosmetics, spread across the dresser top like surgical instruments.

"You can help me if you'd like," she tells Delores. But Delores sits on the bed and watches.

Jill applies red lipstick to the face that has no features.

"Make her smile," Delores says.

Jill scrunches her nose, considering, then shrugs and makes the lips turn up at the corners. She colours in green eyes, with lashes and eyebrows. She paints in a mole with eyeliner, and then she stands back, surveying her work, and adds rouge to the cheeks.

"What do you think?" she asks Delores.

"Pretty," she answers.

"Yeah. Help me dress her."

They go into Bea's closet, find a wraparound skirt, a blouse and a scarf.

Jill cannot wait now for her mother to come home. When Bea finally opens the front door, Delores goes directly to her.

"I didn't do it. Jill did," she says.

Bea kicks off her shoes.

"Show me," she says.

Delores takes her hand and leads her to the master bedroom, Jill follows. She wants to see Bea's reaction.

Bea's breath catches in her throat and she swirls to see Jill behind her. Jill stands with her hands on her hips. Taunting. Jill wants her mother to hit her. She misses her. That's what her body is saying as she leans forward, leans in so close that there is only her and Bea in the room. Hit me, Bea. Go on.

But Bea does not raise her arm.

"Come on, Delores," Bea says instead, stepping back, turning her eyes away from Jill and the smiling mannequin standing in the corner of her bedroom. "How about some toast?"

—

Most of the other kids at school can barely sit still in their seats. School is almost over, it's almost summer, and they can feel the warm wind urging them to run away from the blackboards and tests and teachers. Get outside, run. But Delores does not like the holidays. That's when she is alone all day.

"Remember, do not answer the door, or the phone," Bea always tells her, as she heads out to work.

"Jill, you watch out for her," Bea will say every day, although it's clear Jill doesn't stay home with Delores. Once she's let her sister in after school, she takes off. Delores has told Bea this, but Bea does not want to hear it and so she doesn't.

"Stupid," Jill will say to Delores. "Why don't you just go out and play with your friends? She'll never know."

"I don't want to," Delores says. She doesn't really have friends. She doesn't like climbing or running or skipping, and often sits watching the other kids at recess. During the summer she falls into a lethargy that is like hibernation. Delores goes from her bed to the couch, lies down, and with the remote control she flips from talk show to talk show. This is her summer diet. Delores watches men confess to having sex with their mothers-in-law, she sees skinheads who want to rule the world, and she almost flinches when a young woman throws her chair across the screen at a psychologist trying to give her advice about her gambling addiction. Delores watches and does not watch at the same time, lying down. Mostly, she likes the murmur of voices in her living room.

But now Jill has given her the mannequin. Delores names her. She calls her Sally. It's different now; there is someone in the house with her. Delores gets out of bed, and goes into her mother's room.

"Hi, Sally," she says to the mannequin, who smiles back at her. "It's going to rain today."

Delores starts by changing Sally's clothes every day to match the weather. Sometimes she needs a sweater, or an umbrella, or a beret or straw hat that she finds at the top of Bea's closet. She perches at the end of bed and talks to Sally about what she is watching on TV, and when there is food in the house, she eats and eats, sitting cross-legged at her feet. She steals cigarettes from Mr. Findley and has Sally hold them between her fingers, in her one good hand.

Even Jill starts calling the mannequin by name.

"How's it going, Delores?" she says, appearing in the late afternoons. "What are you and Sally up to? What did you do today?"

"We're playing," Delores says, smiling. This will be her best summer ever, because of her new friend.

—

There are three wooden chairs on the Warbanskis' stoop this evening, two from the kitchen, and one of the good upholstered chairs from the dining room, for their son, Joseph Jr., who's called Joey. The Warbanskis don't believe in wasting good money on plastic lawn furniture.

Joey drove over here as soon as his mother called.

"But that poodle, Fifi, she wouldn't hurt a fly," he's saying, shaking his head. "Just last week I stopped to pat her on the head, and she kind of snuggled up against me."

"She likes pork chops," Anna Warbanski says.

"You've been feeding that dog? They didn't want us to give her bones," her husband Joseph says.

"Well, a bone to chew on never hurts," she answers in a tone that says that's settled.

"But who on earth would do such a thing? Poisoning dogs, in broad daylight?" Joey presses.

"There are people," his father answers.

"What people? Who?" Joey insists.

His father shakes his head. What would his son Joey know of the people on earth who would do such things, Joey, born and raised here on Glendale Avenue in Oakwood? A school teacher now, he went to the university. A good boy.

"Well," Mr. Warbanski says. "How is your car running?"

"Wait, Dad. I'm not sure I like the idea of this, some guy skulking around the neighbourhood with poison, right next door to you. Maybe we should talk about that. You aren't so young now."

"We don't have a dog," his mother points out.

"Still," Joey says.

"It's time." Mrs. Warbanski nudges her husband's foot, leaning over to look at his watch.

They both stand, lifting their chairs.

"Time for what?" Joey says, thrown off his point.

"Oh," his mother says vaguely, "time to make some coffee. Come on, bring your chair."

The Warbanskis go around to their back door, Joey trailing his parents.

A couple of minutes later The Walker, in her yellow jacket, comes out of her house across the street. As soon as Joseph heard that Fifi and Cody were dead, that they were poisoned, he said to his wife "enough." He will not sit on his front step when The Walker is out. His wife now watches the clock, warning him three times a day, and they go inside.

—

Laurel is lying next to Brian, watching the pink smudge spread across the sky through the slats of the bedroom blind. She has barely slept all night. Her mind is going in an endless loop, her back and neck are rigid with tension, and now, at dawn, she's reached a decision.

"Brian, wake up." She pokes him in the side. He grunts and shifts.

"Bri." She leans over, rubbing his back.

He turns, eyes cracking open and stares at the ceiling. "What?"

"I'm going to Victoria. With the kids," she says.

"What?" he repeats.

"I've got it all planned out. I can leave this morning."

"You aren't making any sense, Laurel. You mean, British Columbia? We can't afford plane tickets." He starts to turn back towards his indented pillow, towards sleep.

"I'm driving," she says. "I'm taking the car."

"Hmmm?"

"You can use a company car for a few days."

Brian yawns. "We'll talk about it at breakfast, okay?" He yawns again, eyes drifting shut.

Laurel watches the sky take on a purple, bruised look. She needs to get to the ocean. It's that simple. She is going. All night, the lapping waves teased the edges of her bed, a soft murmur so soothing and real she can taste salt at the back of her throat. Her grandmother retired to Victoria. It won't cost much, just gas really. Laurel is going.

By the time Brian wakes up to shower at seven, Laurel is packed. One suitcase of clothes for her and the kids, that's all. Another suitcase of diapers and baby wipes and a laundry basket filled with red sand pails and shovels. Laurel is moving with the buzzed efficiency of someone who has been up all night. She's running on adrenaline. Sleeping bags and pillows are piled in the car. She's fed the baby, whose blue eyes now watch her from the car seat perched on top of the kitchen counter.

"Good," Laurel says, when Brian comes into the kitchen, stretching. "Now that you're up I'll wake Kayla and Jamie so you can say good bye."

"Laurel." He steps closer, takes her upper arms. "You are not tearing across the country, across the mountains, with three kids in the car."

"Yes, I am," she says.

"What's wrong?" His arms have come around her. He is rubbing her back.

Laurel is blinking hard. The salt taste is getting stronger.

"I need to go to the ocean," she says. "The kids have never been in the ocean."

"It's the dogs. Listen, we're all rattled about it, about..." He pauses, searching. "...these killings. It'll pass." He's rocking her now. Andrea gurgles in her seat, sucking on her pacifier.

Laurel can feel some of the tension ease from her shoulders, but her determination remains.

"Thank you, Brian." She closes her eyes, rests against his shoulder. Then she steps out of his arms. "I want to be on the road by eight."

His eyes narrow.

"Leave the kids," he says.

"No."

"Stop it, Laurel."

"No." She is used to these battles of will with her husband. She always wins. She is stronger than him. It is one of the reasons she hates him, because she thought she was getting a man she could respect when she married him. A dentist's son. But Brian caves into her and then she does things she doesn't want to do. He is supposed to stop her. That's what Laurel thinks. He is supposed to fix things. Fix her. But he doesn't.

"I'll bump my holidays. You fly out today, take the baby, and the kids and I will join you," he says.

Laurel walks past him, shakes Kayla and Jamie awake.

"Come say bye bye to Daddy," she's saying, her voice overly cheerful. "We are going on a big trip now. To the ocean."

Jamie is crying. He hates being shaken awake. It confuses him.

"I don't wanna. I don't wanna," he whines.

Laurel herds the kids, crooning to them in low tones, but Jamie can feel her hands are brisk and steely as she dresses him, not to be messed with. She gets them into the car, with a banana and snack pack of orange juice in their laps. The baby is buckled into her car seat.

Laurel backs their black Caprice out of the garage and down the driveway at two minutes to eight. Brian is leaning heavily against the front door jamb watching as they pull out.

—

It is too scorching a June day for a black car with no air conditioning to be moving west across the naked prairie. Laurel has all the windows rolled down, and maps and children's books are flapping in the hot wind. Laurel is happiest when in motion. She's happy driving. She's making this an adventure.

"Your turn, Jamie. I spy..."

"I spy," he repeats.

"With my little eye," she prompts.

"I spy with my little eye, something," Jamie looks out of the window, searching, but it's been the same for hours, squares of blue, yellow and green. He's used up all of those.

"Look for something inside the car," Laurel tries.

"Blue," Jamie says.

"I know, I know," Kayla bounces in her seat. "The blanket."

"Nope."

"The map."

"No." Jamie giggles.

"The rattle," Laurel offers.

"No."

"We give up," Laurel says.

"The sky," Jamie chortles.

"You can't." Kayla is instantly annoyed. "Mom."

"It doesn't matter," Laurel says.

"But he already said the sky." Kayla is working herself into a rage.

"He's only little, Kayla. Let's play a different game now," Laurel says.

"No, no, no." Kayla is crying at the blinding sun, the sticky seats, the tepid juice.

"Where is the ocean?" Jamie says at a higher pitch than Kayla's crying.

"Two more sleeps," Laurel answers.

"I want to swim now. I'm hot," Jamie demands, and Laurel gives up.

"Mommy, I need to pee," Kayla whines.

"Can you wait a few minutes?" Laurel tries.

"I need to pee, too."

Laurel gives up. She puts on the blinkers and pulls onto the gravel road, hot air settling on them like a blanket as she struggles to get seat belts off and find baby wipes under the mound of junk in the trunk. Jamie stands importantly by the car and pees into the field.

"I don't want to go here. I want a bathroom." Kayla is still whining with that high-pitched, over-tired voice. Andrea bangs her rattle against the inside of the door.

Laurel sits down by the side of the road and starts to laugh. She laughs so hard she is almost sobbing.

"What's wrong, Mommy?" Jamie says, anxious. He puts his little hand, still chubby with baby fat, on her leg. She looks up and sees his face etched with worry.

Laurel breathes deeply, looks up at the sky.

"Mommy's okay now," she says, taking charge.

She kisses Jamie's hand then promises Kayla a Freezee at the next gas station, as long as she pees now.

Jamie gets into the car and promises not to look, so Kayla finally squats by the road and pees.

Laurel gets them buckled back into their seats, and before any new commotion can start up, she reaches over, flicks on the radio, finds a country and western station, and cranks up the volume. She is going down the highway, eating up Saskatchewan.

Even though her hair is pulled back, it's tangled in damp clumps that will be impossible to comb. Kayla murmurs to her Barbie until sleep finally comes. Jamie gives in to the hot wind and nods off, head bobbing against his chest. The baby is like Laurel; she loves the car, and alternates between deep sleep and wide-eyed alertness, studying the world whizzing past without blinking.

Laurel snaps off the radio once they are asleep and almost moans at the sudden, hurting silence. She feels drugged by the heat rising from the asphalt in shimmering waves, as though trying to trick her into believing she's already reached the ocean. The waves are breaking over her black car, glinting in her windows.

She has no word for the thing she catches glimpses of from the corner of her eye, a presence so strong that when it's not there, it's absence is just the same. Laurel's grandmother would nod and say, "that's God, dear." But that is a vocabulary Laurel does not own, and so she drives over the Saskatchewan-Alberta border, speeding towards something she can taste but cannot name.

# CHAPTER 6

The reporter who knocks on Brian's door is young and pretty, and she has a cameraman by her side. Brian has arrived home early from work. News of the dead dogs is on all the radio stations, and all day long people have been asking him what's going on in Oakwood. He finally gives up and drives home in his rented car.

"I'm Sherry Adams." She smiles at Brian.

"I don't really have anything to say." Brian is already closing the door.

"I'm not rolling," she says quickly.

Brian hesitates.

"Listen, police say this is likely an inside job. You know, a chronic complainer who hates dogs. Or someone in the neighbourhood who's not quite right. Do you know anyone like that?"

Instinctively, Brian's eyes move past the reporter, to The Walker's ramshackle wooden house.

"No," Brian says. But Sherry Adams has already made a mental note. Check the white house.

"Thank you,"she says.

She turns and taps her way down the stairs.

"First we go next door," she tells her cameraman. "One of the dogs," she checks her notepad, "the German shepherd, lived there."

Gary comes to the door, steps outside and closes it behind him.

"I'm so sorry to hear about your loss," she says. Sherry reaches out and puts her hand on Gary's shoulder. She had a German shepherd when she was growing up, she tells him, and even though she had dogs after that, he was her favourite.

"Tell me about Cody," she says finally, and signals to the camera to start rolling.

"Cody was a friend," Gary says, "not just mine, but my two sons', and my wife Madeline's. We had him ten years. He was part of our family." Gary is calm and composed and caring.

"How did you find out?" Sherry asks.

"The neighbour next door." He points to Brian and Laurel's house, and swallows hard. "They were having a barbecue and they could tell something was wrong. Cody was making noises. Like he was choking. Brian came over to get me, but by the time we got Cody to the vet, it was too late. He's a big dog to move. He was." Gary looks away. His face creases.

"Take your time," Sherry says.

"His eyes were wild. He didn't want us to put him in the car. I guess he knew he was dying," Gary says.

Sherry is making sympathetic, encouraging sounds in her throat.

"And how do you feel?" she asks Gary. The camera zooms in for a close-up.

"My family is devastated," is what Gary says.

But Gary is not devastated. Gary is thinking about the strange sense of release that has taken hold of him. How he has been tense, and waiting for something to happen ever since the attic.

He knew he was going to pay for those minutes he spent with Laurel. Cody, he knows, is the price. His companion who walked with him for ten years is dead. Gary turns to his wife and children, offering comfort, and they are staying up late into the night, talking at the kitchen table. The family balance is restored. But Gary feels he has killed Cody, the same as if he poured the poison down his throat.

Gary does not say any of this on TV.

"Do you have a picture of Cody that we could have?" Sherry asks. "You know, so our viewers can see him. "

"Yes. Just a second. "

The picture Gary comes back with is of his sons Jake and Curtis with Cody, at the lake. The dog is in the foreground with a stick in his mouth.

"Thank you," Sherry says. "You have been such a help. All of our viewers extend their sympathies to you and your family."

She motions to the cameraman. "Now we go to that house." She points and starts heading towards The Walker's.

"What is she doing now?" Phoebe whispers to Jill. They are under the front steps of Brian and Laurel's house, and since they got home from school an hour ago they have been tailing the reporters who are zigzagging their way up and down Glendale Avenue. They have decided to stick with Sherry because she is the prettiest. Phoebe is trying to scribble facts in their book, but it is more exciting to watch than it is to write, so she's just about given up.

"Quick." Jill pokes her. "It's the teenagers."

Sherry Adams is out in the middle of the street and Tom and Luc and Stretch have come out of Tom's house.

"Hey," Tom calls. Sherry waits, and the light on the camera clicks on. Jill and Phoebe walk nonchalantly to the curb, sit down, and pretend they are not there. Seeing the teenagers this close up does not happen often.

"Hey," Tom says again, reaching them. "What channel are you?"

"Eyewitness News," Sherry says.

"Well, my dog is dead." He's angry, glaring directly into the camera. "Do you know who did this?"

"No." Sherry moves in closer. "Tell me about your dog."

Jill and Phoebe watch Tom's two friends, who are shuffling their feet, saying nothing. Tom talks about Baxter, how strong, how smart his dog is. And now Phoebe is leaning forward, pinching Jill. She cannot believe it, but Tom is crying. He is telling Sherry about the first trick that Baxter mastered, kind of like rolling over but more complicated, and he's stopped talking, because he's fifteen and summer is just starting and his dog is dead and it won't be a summer at all without Baxter. He is choking on his sobs. Luc and Stretch step forward, put their arms around his shoulders, shielding him from the camera, turning their backs, leading him away. Phoebe and Jill watch the three teenage boys, arms around each other, moving at an awkward lope down Glendale Avenue. They can hear Tom's muffled sobs for a long time.

Phoebe puts her hand over her own eyes and finds that her cheeks are wet. She had no idea a teenager, a teenage boy, could cry. Now she sees them all differently. She's all mixed up, and it hurts in her chest.

"Look at her," Jill says.

The reporter Sherry is trying to redo her make-up because her mascara is smudged by tears. Jill watches this with a critical eye. The reporter is not very good, not as good as Bea when it comes to make-up.

Finally, Sherry puts away her compact mirror and keeps walking.

She's on her way to the white house but she needs to find a good place to do her live hit at the top of the newscast. She lights a cigarette, and walks up Glendale Avenue again, waving to several reporters she knows who are also here knocking on doors. The picture of Cody with the stick in his mouth will appear on three TV newscasts tonight, and it will be on the front page of two morning newspapers.

"Joseph, look at this," Mrs. Warbanski says. She is standing behind her filmy white curtains, in the front parlor. Several reporters have knocked at their front door but the Warbanskis do not answer.

"What?" her husband says, from the kitchen, where he is listening to a ball game on the radio.

Mrs. Warbanski is shaking her head.

"You should see them," she says. But Joseph does not bother getting up. Mrs. Warbanski is shaking her head because Sherry is strolling up and down the street in platform shoes smoking cigarettes in broad daylight, like a hussy. In her day, Mrs. Warbanski knows, that would have been enough to ruin a girl. Now look at them. They let them go on the television.

Sherry shades her eyes with her hand and squints. It's perfect. She'd forgotten Oakwood had this. There is a cemetery here at the end of the street, with leafy trees and the river behind it. Death is stalking Oakwood today, she's already writing in her head for her opening sequence. It's ideal, no, too heavy. She'll change it, but she loves the visuals. The cemetery will speak for itself. There is a spring in her step as she heads towards the gates.

"Hello," a voice calls cheerfully to her, from somewhere above her. She has to squint again, looking up.

"Over here," the man calls. It's Gus Gustafson, who lives in the last house on the street before the graveyard.

"I recognize you," he says to Sherry, who is walking to the yard with the rose bushes. "I watch you every night. Hang on. Don't go away."

Gus Gustafson is almost at the top rung of the ladder propped up against the side of his house.

"What are you doing?" Sherry asks.

"Don't go away," he says again, and concentrates now as he swings himself up onto his roof. There is something heavy hanging around his neck, she can see. He grunts and settles himself on the roof.

"You are Sherry Adams, Eyewitness, right?" he says.

"Yes," she says.

"Great. This is great. I always watch you guys. You are my station."

"Thank you. What are you doing up there?" she asks again.

"Videocam," he says, pulling the camera from around his neck. "We don't get a lot of excitement in this part of Oakwood. Just wanted to make sure I get it on tape, for the grandkids."

Gus has the camera going now. He's panning up and down the street. When he gets to Sherry, standing in his front yard, he zooms in, just like a professional.

"Okay, wave now," he calls down to her. "You are on. Can you tell us what you're doing here?" he prompts.

Sherry smiles charmingly, and starts recapping the events of the day in Oakwood, all while walking slowly to the rosebush so the Gustafsons will have a better background when they show off their home video to family and friends and neighbours. He keeps the camera steady, propping it on his knee, panning with her.

"How's that?" she calls up when she's completed her monologue.

"You are the best," he says gratefully.

"If you climb up there at six, you'll be able to film our satellite van," she says. "We'll be stationed right there." She points to the graveyard gates.

"I'll do that," he says. "Wave again."

"Bye bye," she says, waving.

———

"Oh no," Phoebe says, "She's going to The Witch's house."

It is 4:20.

Margaret is inside her home, and she knows they are coming towards her, she can see them coming up the walk. The cameraman is filming her yard. She is already standing in her yellow rain jacket. Her eyes find the clock. Six minutes, and then she has to leave. She has six minutes. She stands in her hallway, listening to the knocking over and over again on her front door.

Jill and Phoebe are so sure The Witch will not come to her door they don't even have to sneak close. But Sherry isn't leaving. She's posing on The Witch's front steps.

"We better get over there," Jill says.

"Let's cut through the side bushes. It's faster," Phoebe says. The side bushes are riskier, because they are not very thick and normally the girls would not dream of being so obvious. But this is not a normal day in Oakwood.

"...the first bridge," Sherry is saying to her cameraman.

Jill looks at Phoebe, who shrugs her shoulders.

"Here in Oakwood," Sherry says.

"Wait. There's a cloud," the cameraman says. They wait for the lighting to get better.

It is 4:23.

The Walker is pressed against the wall in her hallway, listening to the slow tick of her grandfather clock. Her palms are sweating.

"Okay." The cameraman signals.

"Here in Oakwood," Sherry starts again.

"Your hair," the cameraman says.

"Damn." Sherry runs her hand through her shoulder length, chestnut hair. "I knew this cut was going to be trouble. I shouldn't have gone for it."

The Walker has no choice.

It is 4:26, and she has to go now.

She swings open her front door, head down. She's almost running Sherry over by the time the cameraman is rolling again, just in time to capture her shoving past them.

"So sorry to bother you," Sherry is saying, her microphone thrust out.

"No comment," The Walker says. She has been saying this line over and over to herself, in the hallway, for six minutes.

"No comment, no comment, no comment." She's chanting now, and she keeps moving. Only when she's at the bottom of her stairs does her gaze turn sharply, catching Jill and Phoebe. The girls are trying to press further back into the bushes, but it's too late.

The Witch nods at them, once. Then she keeps going.

"I think she just cursed us," Phoebe whispers urgently to Jill.

"No, she didn't," Jill says.

"I want to get out of here," Phoebe says. "Let's go to The Nest."

"You are such a baby," Jill says, and laughs. It's not her high, nervous giggle anymore. Jill laughs deeper, like an adult. Phoebe notices this, and glances quickly. Out of the corner of her eye, Phoebe can see Jill's lips are thin and she looks like Bea. Jill suddenly looks so much like her mother that Phoebe takes an involuntary step backwards.

"Okay, The Nest," Jill says. They pick their way through the bushes to the back fence, and now they can run across the backyard because The Witch is already gone.

"Get the long shot," Sherry is saying and the cameraman follows The Walker to the street, keeping the yellow jacket in focus until it disappears into the first loop.

"Think she did it?" He turns to Sherry, hoisting the camera off his shoulder.

Sherry shrugs. "I don't know. Hard to say. What do you think?"

The cameraman looks at the sky, scratches a mosquito bite on his neck.

"There's no rain coming," he says finally. "It's an odd thing for her to be wearing."

Sherry checks her watch. She pulls out her cellphone and punches in the numbers.

"We've got everything we need," she says into the phone. "Two of the four dog owners, one of them crying, got the cops, some shocked neighbours. Who's doing the veterinarian? What does he say? Gruesome. Yeah. Yeah, okay, sure. We'll be there in ten minutes. I'll do the voice-over and come back for the live open. I've got the perfect spot picked out."

Sherry turns to the cameraman.

"We've gotta drive fast. Editing suite three. That's Joan, isn't it? Good. I've got one hour and twenty minutes to get back here with the microwave van." She checks her watch again. "One hour, fifteen minutes."

"Let's go." The cameraman and Sherry make their way back to the news car, just as The Walker passes on her second loop.

"Phoebe, Phoebe." It is Mr. Gustafson. He's calling across his driveway and motioning with his hand. "Come here."

Phoebe groans, but she turns away from The Nest.

"We gotta," she says to Jill. "C'mon. They talk to my mother all the time."

The girls trudge towards Gus Gustafson, who is staring into the tiny screen at the back of his videocam.

"You must see this," he says when they join him. "It is history unfolding here, right now."

The girls peer into the video screen as he replays the footage he has taken so far.

"Wow," says Jill.

"That is really good. Look at Sherry," says Phoebe.

"How about if I interview you?" Gus says. "Then you can be part of this tape."

"No," Jill answers instantly and starts backing away. "Thank you," she adds politely.

"I'll do it," says Phoebe. She does not want to miss being in the history of her neighbourhood. She thinks Mr. Gustafson is right. Besides, her dad does this practically all the time, on every family vacation and Christmas. It's no big deal.

"Okay, Phoebe," Gus says, pointing the camera. "What's going on here today?"

"Hmm, some dogs are dead. Cody and..." She pulls at her T-shirt, suddenly nervous.

"That's okay, go on."

"...uh, that's all really. Oh and Tom's dog, Baxter. They are going to be on TV tonight for sure."

"What do you feel about this, as Oakwood citizens?" Gus prompts.

Jill is almost at the end of the driveway. She's straining to get away from this.

Phoebe is uncertain what the question means, and a small frown wrinkles her forehead as she thinks. "Well, I feel bad. I guess citizens and dogs have the same rights. And..." She looks around quickly for Jill, needing her support, but Jill is far away.

"That's okay," Gus says, lowering the camera. "You did great, Phoebe. Thanks. Say hi to your mother."

"Okay." Phoebe waves and gets away as fast as she can.

"That was dumb," Jill says.

"You could have helped me," Phoebe snaps back.

"Well. Come on already," Jill says heading back into the cemetery. They take the long way around, looping slowly around the graveyard's gravel roads. It is such an unusal day in Oakwood, who knows what else may have happened? But there are no new graves to report. Only a gathering of large black crows, bickering overhead. Finally they arrive at The Nest.

—

Jill and Phoebe are lying on their stomachs, inside their bush. Phoebe is writing furiously in their book, trying to catch up.

"What should I say about the teenagers?" she asks Jill.

"Sissies," Jill says.

Phoebe punches her in the arm.

"Well, they are," Jill says. "Did you write in there what Sherry was wearing? I love her skirt."

"Not yet."

"Where are the cigarettes?" Jill says.

"What?"

It is Jill now who punches her in the arm.

"You stole them. You smoked them without me."

"No, I didn't," Phoebe says.

"Did, too. They were right here. The matches are gone, too." Jill's voice is hard. "You are sneaking here alone."

"I swear," Phoebe says.

"I wanted to smoke one," Jill says. Jill and Phoebe have not actually tried smoking yet, but they've had the two cigarettes here, waiting.

"Well, it's not my fault," Phoebe says, angry now herself. "Maybe you've been coming here by yourself," she tosses back.

"No," Jill says.

"Wait." Phoebe's voice changes quickly to wonder. "Look." She's peering through the hole in their bush.

Jill edges closer and their arms and legs blend as they dip their heads together, the argument dissolving.

A minivan is pulling into their graveyard, stopping a stone's throw from The Nest. Jill and Phoebe almost give up breathing at the unexpected thrill of it, wriggling so they both can see through the branches. Phoebe will be home late for supper. She knows her mother will not like this, but she doesn't care. This is worth it, even if she is grounded.

The van is equipped with a pizza-size satellite dish on top. Phoebe will call it a giant frisbee when she writes all this down later. The side of the van says CXL-TV: YOUR EYES ON THE WORLD.

Sherry Adams jumps out of the van with her microphone, positioning herself so the headstones and the river will fill the TV screen behind her. She's talking to herself, pacing, practising her live opening.

"Ten minutes," a male voice calls from inside the van. Phoebe reaches over and squeezes Jill's hand. Phoebe is struggling with that terrible urge to giggle. It's welling up inside her, but it would give them away. She has to dig her thumb hard into a jagged pebble until it hurts, just to stop herself.

Mr. Gustafson comes into view. He's glowing with sweat and almost panting.

"Sorry," he says, taking a deep breath. "Don't mean to disturb you. Sherry, could you move about five feet to the left? There's a tree blocking my sightlines, I tried from all over the roof and can't get you."

"Bob," Sherry calls into the van. "Would it work from here?" She moves, still keeping the headstones and river behind her.

Bob steps out of the van, moves the camera on its tripod.

"Yeah, it's fine," he answers.

"Oh, thank you." Mr. Gustafson is relieved. "It'll be perfect now." He is beaming.

"No problem." She smiles.

"How much time do I have?" Mr. Gustafson calls to Bob.

"Five minutes," he says.

"Gotta run," he says, jogging back through the gates to his ladder. Up to his roof, the videocam waiting to tape Sherry doing her stand-up beside her van.

Phoebe pokes Jill in the ribs.

"That's the satellite thing," she whispers, pointing to the van and the pizza dish. "That's what I was saying. "

"Whatever," Jill says.

But Phoebe is concentrating, staring at the dish, trying to make out the waves rising up to where the stars are, but even squinting, she can't see them.

It is six o'clock.

"Go." Bob is outside now, operating the camera. He points to Sherry, and she takes a deep breath and starts talking. Everyone on Glendale Avenue is watching the TV news tonight, and most are watching Sherry, as she bounces from the graveyard at the end of their street to the satellite fixed in the sky, and then back down into their living rooms.

*Come quick, come quick. That's our driveway on TV. Look how good Gary's new attic looks. He's calling it a loft, you know. That poor Tom, crying like that. Now why did they put her in her raincoat on TV? It makes Oakwood look like it's full of weirdos; she's not that bad really, she's not as crackers as the TV makes her look.*

Everyone is watching the news except Tom. He stomps upstairs, slamming his bedroom door, and he's not answering his phone, either. As soon as the three teenagers get back to Tom's house, and the awfulness of what has happened sinks in, they come up with a plan. Luc calls the TV station. He disguises his voice, pretending he is Tom's father, and says he does not give the TV station permission to use the interview with Tom.

"Tough," says the editor. "Sue us." He's up against a deadline and he recognizes a hoax call when he hears one. He didn't fall off the turnip truck yesterday. Besides, he's seen the raw footage, and it's the best part of Sherry's story, that kid crying.

Tom pulls the pillow over his head. He will stay like that all evening, because the most embarrassing minute of his whole life is on Eyewitness News, and he is never going to school again, ever. His feet are cold. He always let Baxter into his room at night, and they had a deal. Baxter sprawled across the bottom of the bed, and Tom took the top section. Tom would slide his feet under the heavy, warm body. He should have let Baxter in when he got home from school, before supper. He'd heard him barking. New tears are sliding down Tom's cheeks, but this time they are silent and invisible, absorbed by his pillow.

His feet will be cold all night.

———

"And now our lead story continues with the veterinarian who examined Cody," says Sherry, winding up her live report from the graveyard.

"That's it," she says to Bob. "Let's go. I'm starving."

The van doors slide shut and CXL-TV is gone from Oakwood.

Jill and Phoebe crawl out of The Nest, brushing twigs and dirt from their arms and legs, heading for home.

Another reporter takes over from where Sherry left off. The residents of Glendale Avenue learn that four dogs died in Oakwood of strychnine poisoning. It hits a dog quickly following ingestion, causing muscular twitches, a feeling of suffocation, painful spasms. The eyeballs protrude, the pulse becomes rapid, there is foaming at the mouth, death comes after the third or fourth seizure, due to respiratory failure or exhaustion or collapse. It takes about ten minutes for a dog of Cody's size to die, less for a smaller dog. The veterinarian calls it excruciating, one of the most distressing ways to die.

Phoebe's mother turns off the TV, and goes into the backyard. She walks slowly, inch by inch, studying the grass, looking for anything suspicious. She will not let Phoebe's brothers play in the yard this summer. No more camping out in the tent, either. That's it, no arguments.

The residents of Glendale Avenue do not sleep well tonight.

———

It is Tom's father who drags him out of bed in the morning and makes him go to school. He can't even skip out because his father always insists on driving him right to the door, and waits until he goes inside. Like he's a baby. Sometimes Tom just hates his father.

Tom gets in the car, hunching into the seat, knees up against the glove compartment, baseball cap pulled low over his eyes.

His father starts the car.

"Tom, about Baxter," he says.

"I don't wanna talk about that," Tom says quickly, and he's fumbling around his seat, grabbing his Walkman because he's going to check out of this scene, like fast.

His father clears his throat, does not look at Tom even by accident when he is changing lanes, and he starts again.

"I think it's time we got your beginner's license," he says. "We could go out driving this summer. You know, get the feel of the car."

Tom stops fiddling with the Walkman.

"You'll be sixteen soon. I guess you'll be needing your license," his father adds. "I thought we could go get your beginner's permit this week."

"I guess," Tom says, "if you want." He looks out the window the rest of the way to school. He does not put on his Walkman. It stays in his lap.

Stretch and Luc are hanging around the front door when Tom gets to school. It's not like they are waiting for him or anything, but as soon as Tom gets there they go through the doors as a trio, slouching and glaring, preparing to do battle.

At morning assembly, a girl in Tom's class brushes up against him.

"Sorry about your dog," she says. "I have a Doberman. You can walk him with me sometime, if you like."

Tom is so stunned by this he mumbles an idiotic "'kay, sure" and the tips of his ears go hot. All day long, girls are crossing the hall to talk to him, even the good-looking ones. They're leaning against his locker at lunch and one slips him a note during French class, written all in French so he has to take it home and look up the words. It seems crying on TV isn't half-bad. He's a walking chick magnet. Even Luc and Stretch, glimpsed vaguely next to Tom on the news, now warrant nods of recognition from the girls as they swing their pierced navels down the hallway. Tom would give up all the girls to have Baxter back, that goes without saying. But still.

# CHAPTER 7

Laurel wakes up stiff and cramped in the front seat of the car, sitting up slowly so she won't wake the baby. She pulled into this Kamloops motel parking lot so late last night, she didn't know it overlooked a ravine. The mountains ringing her are like middle-aged men with shiny, receding foreheads, just bristles of trees sticking up on top. In the grey half-light, a magpie flits from tree to dusty earth, flashing black and white.

Laurel gets out of the car carefully, locking the doors behind her, rolling her shoulders and neck.

"I could use a bathroom," she says to the clerk on duty at the motel's front desk.

"For paying customers only," he says.

He's about eighteen, not that much younger really than Laurel, but right now she feels a hundred years older. She really has to work to muster up her usual charm.

She leans nonchalantly on the counter. "You must be the manager," she says, and looks at him appreciatively.

"Not really. I mean, no. I'm the night clerk."

"You are used to making decisions, I can see that." Laurel nods. "I like a man who is comfortable with his authority." She smiles at him.

He reaches for the bathroom key, slides it over the counter.

"Here you go," he says. "Can't hurt."

"Why, thank you." Laurel looks surprised and pleased. "You are the best."

Laurel fumbles with the door, and she can see in the smoked glass and fluorescent light that she is haggard. It was those mountains yesterday, so jagged and forbidding. They had her crawling like a black insect. Laurel was gripping the steering wheel until her knuckles turned white. There was no give to those peaks, those slate walls looking down at her, judging her. The sky in there was nothing but a slit, and the howling wind had almost ripped her door off its hinges when she pulled off the twisted road and stepped out of the car. She wanted to yell something at those mountains, but her voice was carried away, knocked sideways so she did not even get an echo, and she had given up. Every ounce of energy had gone into getting out before dark. Get out, get out, get out. That had held her together, barely.

The clerk at the front desk is waiting with a large, Styrofoam cup of steaming coffee.

"Here," he says, pushing it towards her.

"Thank God," she says to him. "I can go on after all." She takes a sip.

"Hmm. How much?"

"Forget it."

"Thanks, again." Her smile this time is warm and sincere. She slides back into her car and studies the little mounds of sleeping arms and legs in the back seat. She smiles. She is heading towards Penticton now, where Jamie was born, to show him the little house on the edge of town where he started his life. She can make it to Kelowna before the kids wake up.

Laurel is slipping down the highway now in a trance so perfect it is better than a dream. The road cuts through hills that are round and soft as a mother's breasts, so easy after the looming

Rockies that Laurel is tempted to just stop and lay down her head. There are almost no houses and no cars pass her. Through her partially opened window the air is buttery and moist. Cicadas drone and click. Peace seeps through the open window. Laurel is drinking it in with her coffee, driving along this cleavage in the greenish light.

———

Brian feels something cold move in him, a feeling of dread. A moment ago he had been chatting to his neighbours, idly surveying his yard. His gaze rested for a minute on the longish grass that needs cutting and the sprouting marigolds, and then moved on to the garage that needs a serious cleaning. He likes to keep his garage organized. His eyes narrow now as his gaze travels up to the back garage shelf.

"Excuse me," he says suddenly to Gary and Madeline over the fence. Laurel has been gone three days. Gary and his family have just returned from the lake, where they had gone to bury Cody, in back of their cottage.

"Excuse me," Brian says. "I have to go." There is a strange look passing over Brian's face.

Gary raises an eyebrow, and his hand tightens slightly on Madeline's arm.

"Just some stuff I have to check on," Brian says, and he turns, steps into the garage.

"I have to look after some stuff, too," Gary says, relieved.

Brian is walking directly to the back shelf in his garage where he puts items that he does not want in the house near the children. He is focused on the crooked box. He snags the ladder from the corner and climbs up a few steps so he can reach the bottles of paint thinner, bleach, insecticides, weed killer for the lawn, Raid for the ant hills, rat poison.

The box of strychnine is tipped on its side.

"Yes," Brian says out loud, to the garage. "Okay. I knew this." In a quick flash he sees the white dusting of powder, like icing sugar, on the hood of the black car as Laurel is backing out of the driveway with the kids, heading West. It had registered; Brian had seen it and then looked away. He cannot look away now, because there is a film running in his head...he sees the raw hamburger meat on the plate in the fridge, the patties already made up, as he reaches in for his beer; Laurel is hurrying out, walking to the store for hamburger buns. These facts fall into Brian's movie quickly, already edited together into a seamless flow.

The clutch at his throat gives one kick then eases. Brian climbs off the crate and finds a pair of his old work gloves. He searches near the front of the garage until he finds a plastic garbage bag.

"Right," he says to himself. He climbs back up, and with his gloved hands, he takes the fallen box of strychnine and examines it. The top has been ripped haphazardly. It's almost empty. Brian has never opened this box, although he's had it for several years. It was an emergency supply of poison to get rid of problem gophers in another house, when they'd lived on the outskirts of another town.

He carefully drops the box into the garbage bag. Some of the powder has spilled along the shelf, so Brian cleans the shelf thoroughly, sweeping it with his gloves.

He steps down from the ladder and lifts it neatly back into its corner. He puts his gloves into the garbage bag. He looks around for something else to put in the bag to give it some bulk, make it look normal. He adds some newspapers stacked in the recycling box. It is not their garbage day, but Brian knows it is for the people who live across the boulevard. He's not thinking, he's simply moving on automatic pilot, one step at a time. One thing at a time.

Brian steps out of the garage, and into his backyard.

He walks his green bag of strychnine and powdered gloves down the street, across the boulevard, and down a back lane, until he finds a large enough pile of bags in someone's yard to drop his, nonchalantly. He walks a few feet away, turns back. The bag blends perfectly into its surroundings.

"Right," he says again, out loud. "That's done.

———

Laurel is ahead of rush hour traffic as she descends into the valley cradling Kelowna. She shakes her head, trying to reconnect.

It is a weekday. People will be rushing out in suits, going to air-conditioned offices. Laurel is searching for a McDonald's. She's been on the road three days. The first night she checked them into a room. But last night she did not bother because it was so late and the kids were asleep anyway. They just slept in the car. Laurel likes the feeling she gets from arriving late and leaving early; no one knows you've been there.

Laurel shakes her head again, hard. She needs more coffee.

"Three orange juice, one milk and a large coffee," she orders into the metal speaker.

The disembodied voice comes at her. "Coffee with cream and sugar?"

"Yes."

"Drive ahead, please."

Laurel inches forward to the window to pick up her order. Kayla is stirring, Jamie will be awake in a second.

"Manitoba," the woman in the McDonald's window says, reading the Caprice license plate as Laurel approaches.

"Wow, you've come a long way. Where are you headed?" she asks, fishing in the till for the correct change.

"Victoria. Maybe. I'm not sure."

"Well. You're through the worst now, those mountains," the woman says, smiling. "The road ahead is easy."

"Thanks," Laurel says.

"Mommy. McDonald's. Yay!" It is Kayla, instantly alert as she opens her eyes to the hallowed golden arch. She is bouncing in the back seat, jostling Jamie who starts his morning whine.

"Let's get a hamburger," Kayla demands. "I wanna play now."

"Me, too, me, too, I don't want to," Jamie wheedles.

"Got your hands full," says the McDonald's woman, shaking her head sympathetically as she hands over the coffee and juices through the window.

"Yeah," Laurel sighs. "I guess we are coming in."

Laurel parks, untangles the kids from seat belts and car seats and grabs the diaper bag. Balancing Andrea on her hip, bag over her shoulder, coffee clutched in her left hand, she makes Kayla and Jamie walk, not run, across the parking lot.

Laurel buys each of them a Disney's Kim Possible doll, orders Egg McMuffins and drinks her third coffee at the indoor McDonald's play structure. Kayla and Jamie climb and crawl around the Ronald McDonald plastic tubing with their new toys for close to an hour. Laurel sips her coffee and studies Andrea as she plays with the car keys, killing time. She considers striking up a conversation with the other mother watching her kid play. She decides she simply does not have the energy.

Finally Laurel troops the children into the bathroom to wash their hands and faces and pee and brush their teeth. She washes Andrea's arms and legs briskly with paper towels. Andrea kicks at the scratchiness.

Laurel looks up into the mirror and catches an unguarded glimpse of her haggard face. She stares into her eyes until she is forced to blink and turn away.

She does not want to go to the ocean. This comes to her as a complete thought. She cannot imagine why she had wanted to in the first place, how she even came to be heading in this direction. She is now just four hours away from the shore. Her stomach muscles tighten with the certainty that she does not need salt water, or waves, or the sinking submission the ocean demands.

"Come on. We're going. Jamie, stop that," she says automatically. He is amusing himself pulling the paper out of the dispenser.

"I said now." Her voice is louder, firm. Jamie looks up, bottom lip trembling.

"Kayla, hold your brother's hand. We're going to the car."

Laurel hoists the newly diapered Andrea into her arms and begins the long and torturous journey out of McDonald's.

"Animal cookies, Mommy, " Jamie pleads, predictably.

"No. Mommy has no money," Laurel says.

"Mommy, but..."

Laurel stops. She has almost made it to the door. "If you get animal cookies you have to give back Kim Possible to the lady," Laurel says to Jamie. "You pick."

"No," he says defiantly, hugging the toy close.

"That's what I thought. Keep moving," she says.

Laurel has decided she is not going to Penticton, either. She hates that town. An elderly doctor there said she was suffering from postpartum depression after Jamie was born and she could not get out of bed. He wanted her to join a peer therapy group and go for individual counselling. He even spoke with Brian about it. Brian agreed with him. Brian would come home at lunch to find Kayla standing in her crib, crying. Jamie would be in bed with Laurel, wet, with dirty diapers. Laurel could not breast-feed him. Jamie was losing weight. That was the first time Brian went out and hired a mother's helper; not a young girl, but a mature, older woman. Laurel responded by taking the bus to Vancouver and racking up more than $1,000 on their credit card. She bought herself a pink leather mini-skirt and matching pink jacket from the Leather Ranch.

Now, Laurel ignores the turnoff to Victoria. The black car is heading towards Revelstoke.

"Mommy, when do we get to the ocean?" Jamie asks. The kids know today is the day they get to the beach.

"We're not going to the ocean," Laurel says.

"Yes, we are," Kayla pipes in.

"No, we're going home now," Laurel says.

Kayla starts to sniffle. "Mommy, I want to go to the ocean," she insists.

"We don't always get what we want," Laurel says. "Even when we are close. Especially when we are close."

Jamie is whining, too. Laurel is driving towards Revelstoke and promising to stop for a whole afternoon in Alberta so they can see real dinosaur bones. When they get home they can have a day at the water slides, and a trip to Skinners for hot dogs. These treats are to make up for the ocean, ebbing and flowing and pulsing without them.

—

"Phoebe, I want to talk to you about something," her mother says.

"I'm meeting Jill now," Phoebe says, in a rush to be outside. It's finally holidays, no school, and it is hot and beckoning out there.

"Sit down for a second."

Phoebe sits.

"I've enrolled you in camp this year. With the Y. You'll be going to the island for two weeks." Her mother sits back. They battled over this last summer, because Phoebe would not go without Jill.

"But, Mom." Phoebe starts on a whine.

"Canoeing, campfires, swimming lessons, blueberry picking. This isn't punishment, Phoebe, this is fun," her mother says mildly.

Phoebe considers. It does sound fun. On a day like this, to be at the lake instead of stuck here in Oakwood, it does sound good. Last year, she heard about the pillow fights and marshmallows and ghost stories at school, and she'd wished she'd gone.

"What about Jill?"

"I have no control over Jill," Phoebe's mother says. "If you are such good friends, a couple of weeks won't change that, Phoeb."

Phoebe gets a little stab in her side. This is what worries her. She thinks maybe a couple of weeks will change everything. It's all changing now, anyway, with Jill.

"It won't hurt you to play with some other girls your age for a few weeks," Phoebe's mother adds.

"Okay," Phoebe says, fast, before she can change her mind.

"Okay, what?"

"Okay, I'll go." The instant Phoebe says this, she starts getting excited inside.

"We'll go shopping tomorrow and get you a few things, then," her mother says. "There's a list of stuff you need."

"Okay, Mom." She's going to camp. She wants to keep this to herself for a while, savour it. When she meets Jill on the driveway, she doesn't tell her about it right away.

"Too hot for bikes," Jill says. It's only mid-morning and it's already a scorcher. They have to step over a cat lying on the street, belly down and legs splayed, trying to hug the coolness of the shady cement. Unleashed, this cat is breaking the law. It doesn't care. It won't even move for them to get by.

"I know, let's walk to the other side," Jill says, pointing across the river. It's a trip they make from time to time. It's a long hike, but school is out and they have nothing but long days to fill now.

"Good idea," Phoebe says.

They take a break halfway, sitting on the wooden sidewalk of the bridge. They can just squeeze their legs under the railing, swinging their feet free out over the water.

The bridge used to be all grey steel. Now it's a combination of white-green pigeon poop and rusty blotches.

"I'm going to camp," Phoebe says. She keeps her head wedged in one of the open diamond spaces of the bridge, so that she does not have to face Jill.

Jill says nothing. The pigeons coo and flap overhead, and the bridge bucks under the weight of lumbering trucks at their backs.

"Did you hear me?"

"I heard you. Hurray, you're going to camp."

"It was my mother's idea," Phoebe says defensively.

"You'll get lice," Jill says. "Head lice. Those are bugs that make a nest in your hair and crawl around in your ears day and night."

"I will not." Phoebe is angry now.

"Everyone who goes to camp gets lice," Jill says matter-of-factly. This is what Bea told Jill and Delores last summer, when they wanted to know why they couldn't go with the other kids to that camp where they sing songs around a campfire and sleep in bunk beds. Bea did not have the money to send them to camp and she was fed up with them asking. So she told Jill and Delores about the lice. Bea remembered getting lice as a child and scared Jill and Delores with the vivid details.

"You have to soak your head in vinegar for months and months to get rid of them," Jill adds, for good measure.

"Maybe you could come," Phoebe says.

"I don't want to," Jill says. "I'm not even asking. Only babies go to camp, anyway."

The sun is beating down on them. Even the river is too hot to move. It's like melting toffee with little eddies whirling, unable to go backwards or forwards; it's confused. That's what can happen on a prairie day with this kind of sun and humidity and sharp blue sky. The river stops breathing, and waits.

Jill stands up. "You coming?" she says over her shoulder.

Phoebe falls into step with her as they come down off the bridge. It's different over here. There are more stores and restaurants and parking lots.

Jill and Phoebe make their way past Taco Bell and Blockbuster and Shoppers Drug Mart.

"Got any money?" Jill asks.

"No." Phoebe says.

"I got money. From Laurel. See? I'm making lots of money this summer. Who needs camp?" She tosses her ponytail.

"Laurel is gone. My mom said," Phoebe adds.

"I know that. I knew that before you did. Mr. Murray told me," Jill says importantly. "She's coming back in a few days. Then I bet she'll really need lots of help from me."

Phoebe shrugs, kicks a rock.

"Let's get ice cream," Jill says. She relents. "Come on. I'll buy you an ice cream."

Phoebe glances up. "Okay."

They kick the rock back and forth as they walk to the Dairy Queen. They get double chocolate twist cones that are dripping in the heat as fast as they can lick them.

They cut through traffic to the riverbank, where there is a park directly across from their graveyard.

"Looks different from here," Jill says.

"Can you see The Nest?"

"No."

"Me neither."

"Look at the Gustafsons' house," Phoebe says, pointing.

"It's like a doll house," Jill says.

From this bank Oakwood looks thickly green and impenetrable, like a jungle. From here, Glendale Avenue is invisible.

They plop themselves down on the grass in the middle of a stand of poplar trees. Poplars are Jill's favourite because usually they giggle and wave in the breeze, but not today. Today everything is still.

"What do you want to do now?" Phoebe asks lazily. They are lying on their backs, staring through the leaves at the sky. No clouds to twist into pictures today.

"Nothing," Jill says.

They don't talk after that; they just lie side by side, listening to the buzz of a lawn mower in the distance. Phoebe's eyelids feel heavy; they are closing. Jill is counting each separate leaf above her, until the numbers run together, and she half sleeps.

It might be twenty minutes, or two hours, or two years that go by.

It's Jill who sits up first, breaking through the cotton batten that's slipped down, surrounding them. She pushes groggily through the thickness, puts her hand on Phoebe's shoulder and shakes her awake.

"Time to go," she says.

They walk the long way back, because there's more shade that way, but still the sweat drips under their arms and off their foreheads and under their ponytails.

When they get to the top of Glendale Avenue, Jill stops.

"So do you want to ride our bikes tomorrow?" she asks.

"I've gotta go shopping tomorrow," Phoebe says quickly. "With my mom."

Jill turns away, takes a step in the direction of the boulevard. Towards the 7-11, where they aren't supposed to go.

"Why are you going that way?" Phoebe asks, putting out a hand as if to stop her, but she doesn't.

"'Cause I feel like it," Jill answers. "Catch you later, Phoebe."

"Are you mad at me? Because I don't care," Phoebe says, in a rush.

Jill turns back. "Come with me. There are other kids in back of the Sev," Jill says. "It's fun."

"Who?" Phoebe demands.

"Luc. He's cute. Sometimes he's there," Jill says. She doesn't mention the others she has found. The guys who don't even go to school and hang out by the railway tracks. Jill does not tell her about that guy Trip, who dared her to kiss him and put his tongue in her mouth when she said okay.

Phoebe is incredulous. "Luc is fifteen. Do you talk to him?"

Jill kicks a rock, watching as it skitters towards the sewer. "He shares his cigarettes with me," she says finally.

Phoebe takes a step backwards. For a moment Jill and Phoebe look at each other, saying nothing.

"I gotta go now," Phoebe says. She turns and does not look back, does not watch Jill crossing the boulevard, going away from her.

Phoebe makes her way home slowly. She stops at the beach and skips flat rocks on the still surface of the river. One, two, three jumps, then the rock sinks.

She sits down in the grass and looks for a four-leaf clover. She lies back and looks at the clouds, telling herself she doesn't care about Jill and Luc. The ants find her, making her legs itch. Finally Phoebe gives up, admitting it isn't much fun hanging out by herself. She wants to go to camp now, today. She wants Jill to be like before, like last summer, when they would read comics for hours and giggle in The Nest. She walks down Glendale Avenue towards home.

It's a relief to let the screen door slam behind her, sniff the warm kitchen air. It's weird for her mother to be cooking on such a hot day; usually when it's muggy like this, they eat salad and cold ham and watermelon. They'll be sleeping downstairs in the rec room tonight.

"What are you baking?" she calls out to her mother.

"It's not for us. Don't touch it," her mother calls back.

"Banana bread?" Phoebe guesses.

"Coffee cake," her mother says, coming round the corner and into the kitchen, pulling the warm pan towards her.

"Who's it for?" Phoebe asks.

"None of your business. I should be allowed to have a few secrets, don't you think?" her mother says.

"Yeah, right," Phoebe says. The idea of her mother having secrets so is funny she grins at her.

Her mother relents. "I baked it for Margaret." She gently taps the cake out of its pan, searching for aluminum foil.

"Margaret? The Witch, Margaret?" Phoebe is incredulous as she goes to the fridge, and pulls out the jug of Kool Aid.

"I wish you'd stop calling her that." Her mother sighs.

"She won't eat it, Mom," Phoebe says, certain.

"Well, that will be her choice, then. But at least she'll have a choice," her mother answers. Determinedly, she picks up the cake, kisses her daughter on the cheek and heads down Glendale Avenue.

As soon as Phoebe is alone in the house, she runs upstairs to her room. She turns on her mini-stereo and inserts her favourite Avril Lavigne CD. She is teaching herself to dance the way they do on MuchMusic, imitating the videos. She's wearing her training bra and sticking her chest out in the mirror as she sways her hips. Phoebe does not know what she wants, exactly, only that it is taking too long to get here. She pulls out the book from under her bed and under today's date she puts it this way: Life Sucks. Then on the next line she quickly adds, I am going to camp! The Blood Sisters spy book is changing into Phoebe's diary, but that is not the way it was supposed to be. It just seemed to happen when she wasn't looking.

———

Janice is not put off by the overgrown bushes and the peeling paint at the front door of Margaret's house.

This is what happens, if you are all alone in the world, with no kids, or brothers or sisters or man, no relatives of any kind, Janice thinks. It's only natural that this is what happens. Everything decays when it's not tended.

She's knocking on the door, balancing the warm cake on her left arm. She baked coffee cake because it smells like rocking on a front porch with friends. Neither she nor Margaret has a front porch, but it's the smell that matters.

"Margaret," she's calling out. "I know you're there. Come to the door. It's Janice, Phoebe's mother." Knock, knock, knock, pause.

The Walker's heart is pounding like a trapped bird's. When she sees Phoebe's mother turn onto her front walkway, she is scrambling to her kitchen. Not again. Why are they suddenly coming here? And Phoebe's mother won't just go away like that television reporter. This is worse because she can't just say "no comment." She is standing completely still behind the kitchen door, her breath going in and out of her lungs with a soft rasp, as though she's been running.

"For heaven sakes," Janice says under her breath. "This is just so silly." She sighs deeply, and after a few minutes, calling Margaret, Margaret, I'm here to visit, she admits to herself that Margaret knows she is here, and will not come to the door. Janice is upset because there are some on Glendale Avenue whispering about the dogs, pointing to this house. It's not right. Someone has to make an effort, that's all. She bends down, and puts the coffee cake by the door. When she's halfway down the walk, she turns, looks at the peeling house, and sighs again, wiping the sticky sweat off her forehead with the back of her hand. Maybe she should organize a neighbourhood clean-up day, and then volunteers could tackle this place. Some pruning, a quick coat of paint to the front and it could be fine in no time.

Margaret, The Walker, The Witch, knows she is gone.

Still, she waits another twenty minutes, until her heartbeat slows, until her breathing is even and deep and clean. She rubs her wet palms against her thighs. She can hear the ticking of her grandfather clock in the absolute quiet, and so she counts the passing minutes, until it's okay again.

Then she opens her front door, and carries the warm cake into her dining room, clearing a spot for it on the oak table. She pushes aside the packages that keep arriving: tortoise shell sunglasses, a platinum pendant in a rosewood box, a sonic toothbrush, a case of barbecue sauce although she does not own a barbecue and rarely eats meat.

She pushes all this aside, and opens the card stuck to the top of the coffee cake.

*To Margaret,* it says, *From Janice, Gordon, Phoebe, Brad and Gordie: 22 Glendale Avenue.*

Margaret goes to the rolltop desk, and in the bottom drawer she finds the notepaper she is looking for. She remembers precisely how to do this, from her days at private school. She finds her black fountain pen and uncaps it. She's frowning in concentration.

The note paper is already engraved in gold embossed letters, *From the home of Margaret Sutherland.* She writes, laboriously but with perfect penmanship, *Thank you so much for the wonderful gesture. I really appreciate your taking the time to bake and deliver this delicious coffee cake. Sincerely, Margaret Sutherland.*

She will ask the mailman to deliver this note for her tomorrow. *To Janice and family,* the envelope says simply. Margaret is aware of the adults who watch her when she is out walking, but it is the neighbourhood children that catch her interest. They follow her on their bikes and rollerblades, and they don't seem to realize she listens as she walks. She knows all the children's names and ages and who's got a crush on whom, and who's staying for another detention at school and who is smoking cigarettes. Phoebe and Jill follow her deliberately and she knows them best of all.

Margaret cuts herself a large slab of the coffee cake and puts it on a Wedgwood plate, pushing up the frayed sleeves of her sweatshirt. Phoebe is wrong, because she does eat it. It is delicious. Margaret releases the mute button on her TV, which she pressed when she saw Janice turn into her yard. She's watching the shopping channel, as always.

———

Laurel does not breathe again from deep down in the bottom of her lungs until she crosses over the Saskatchewan border. She should be looking for a motel, but the sun is sinking in an explosion of orange dust. It is filling her rear-view mirror, tempting her to turn around, stop. *Just stop, Laurel.* What voice is that, whose?

Laurel slows, nudges the car off the highway. She makes a U-turn onto the gravel shoulder, facing west.

The yellow carpet of canola stretches as far as the eye can see. There is just a tease of purple-blue flax in the distance. There is so much room to breathe now, Laurel is almost drowning in air.

"Mommy, Mommy, Mommy," Kayla says.

"Not now, honey. Just a minute."

"Mommy, I spy," Kayla goes on.

Laurel cannot hear her. She puts a hand against her window, where the orange is bleeding into peach. The sky, so huge and open and waiting for her to... what? She should not have stopped the car. It is better to keep driving. Now the question hammers inside her head and she already knows she will not get an answer, because she never does. Laurel strains forward against her seat belt to meet the soft brilliance, fingers stroking the window, stroking the sky.

"Mommy," Kayla says, louder.

Laurel finally sits back. Her hand lets go of the warm pinks and drops onto the steering wheel.

"What is it? What do you spy?" Laurel asks her.

"Nothing," Kayla says. "It's gone."

———

Brian is mowing the front lawn the next day when the black car swings into the driveway at suppertime. They have been gone seven nights, eight full days.

Jamie and Kayla are scrambling out of the back seat, bare feet turning green as they fly over the freshly cut grass to leap against their father.

"And we saw..." Jamie is panting.

"A deer," Kayla says.

"A goat with horns," Jamie says.

"It was a sheep that lives in the rocks," Kayla corrects, importantly.

"We had McDonald's three times."

"And last night the mosquitoes were as big as damn horseflies," Jamie says. He sounds so exactly like Laurel as he says this, Brian laughs out loud. Over their heads, he watches Laurel, standing on the driveway with the baby on her hip.

"I called your grandmother," he says. "She told me you changed your mind. That you never made it to Victoria."

"I wanted to come home," she says.

"I was worried, Laurel. You must have known that." His voice is calm but Laurel knows he is angry. He gets very quiet when he is angry.

She looks away, shifts Andrea to her other hip.

"And was it worth it?" he asks.

"Don't ask me questions like that, Brian. You know better." She starts to turn away. He walks across the lawn, Kayla and Jamie clinging to his side. He stops just in front of her, his hand cupping her chin.

"Laurel?"

"Yes?"

"Is there anything you want to tell me about?" His eyes are steady on hers.

She shrugs. "No."

He nods, turns and picks up Jamie, holding Kayla's hand to go inside.

Later that night, when everyone is asleep, he quietly opens the screen door. The neighbourhood seems so still now, without the occasional dog barking. Brian has taken to sitting on his front steps late at night, sipping two fingers of scotch. He's listening to the tinkle of wind chimes from the house across the street, wafting over on the summer breeze.

He thinks about Laurel.

His parents would say, "Well, what did you expect? You married her because she was pregnant. And she lies, she always did. We told you. So what if she's pretty, Brian? Think." That's what they said; it is what they still say. He did get Laurel pregnant, but he didn't marry her because of that. He is with Laurel because he loves her. It's a simple fact. She can't help it if she has episodes, Brian thinks, and he can't help loving her. Laurel and Brian have packed up and moved four times in the six years they have been married. It will get harder to keep doing this, once all the kids are in school. But for now, Laurel is clever enough to keep outrunning herself, with Brian's help.

She's in the doorway, interrupting his thoughts. "Brian."

He looks up, sees her through the screen.

"Are you coming to bed?" she asks.

"Yeah, I am," he says, and he gets up, goes inside.

If Brian had stayed outside another half-hour, listening to the wind chimes, he would have seen them coming.

———

"Got a smoke?" the teenager says to his buddy.

"Left 'em in the car," he answers.

"Stupid." The first one pushes against him, half punching his arm. But he's laughing.

"Yeah. This way."

They are coming down the back lane towards Glendale Avenue, both wearing black windbreakers, baggy pants and running shoes. One wears a baseball cap backwards. It is one o'clock in the morning and dead quiet in Oakwood.

"Guess we need us another car," the taller one says.

"Got that right. Your turn."

The second one laughs now, too.

"It's always my turn, man."

They are teenagers, and they are sick of walking. A couple of hours ago they'd had a cool car they'd picked up in the west end of the city but they'd spotted cops. They couldn't tell if the cops had spotted them, so they ditched the Mazda near the Disraeli Freeway just in case.

The tall one is working now, while his partner watches the street for movement. It is a good street because many of the houses do not have garages equipped with those annoying motion detector lights. The cars are in plain view. They move down Glendale Avenue trying the car doors, looking for one that's unlocked. They will steal a car either way, but it's easier if it's already unlocked. They like easy. No luck.

"Pissing me off," says the first one.

"We need cash anyway," says the second. He leans down, pulls the hunting knife from the leather sheath tucked into his sock, held there against his shin by an elastic band.

"Here." He motions with the glinting blade. "This one. We'll get the keys. Maybe even smokes."

The blade is pointing at the Warbanskis' house. Joseph's new, navy blue Buick Century is parked in the driveway. The teenagers peg it as an old man's car, an easy mark. They saunter towards the back door.

# CHAPTER 8

Joseph and Anna Warbanski hear the banging at the back door in the middle of the night, and come awake slowly, dazed. Joseph is up, turning on the lamp, pulling on the thick robe his son Joey bought him last Christmas.

"Don't answer," Anna says groggily, rubbing at her eyes.

"Yeah, yeah," he says, already making his way down the hall, through the kitchen. The pounding is louder here. Someone must be in trouble, he thinks, at this hour.

He unlocks the deadbolt and opens the door a crack, trying to see around it, out into the dark.

"Wha..." he starts. With one hard shove, the teenagers are in. Joseph stumbles backwards, almost knocked down by the force of the door as it slams into his shoulder. He fights to keep his balance, reaching to brace himself against the wall. Two large shapes loom over him. He blinks hard, trying to bring the black windbreakers into focus in the dim hallway.

"Don't do nothin' stupid, old man," says one of them.

Joseph catches sight of a glinting blade. He feels a rush of anger when he sees the knife.

"Get out, you can't... Get out," he says forcefully, loudly.

From her bed, Anna hears Joseph has raised his voice. A cold, quick grip in her chest tells her to stay quiet. Her heart begins to pound too hard, making her almost dizzy. She lies back, under the covers, unsure if she should stay in this room or go to Joseph. She's paralyzed, already knowing it does not matter what she does.

The second teenager steps closer and raises his fist, punching Joseph hard on the side of the head. Joseph staggers.

"Shut up," he says.

"You alone in here?" the first one, the one with the knife, demands.

Joseph has a ringing in his right ear, and a hot flush spreads outwards over his cheek, down to his jaw. He shakes his head, trying to clear away the hollow buzzing.

"Yes," he says. Then, hoping Anna will hear him, he says it again louder. "I am alone here. Get what you want and go."

"Good. Shut up, get out of our way, and you don't get hurt. Got it?"

Joseph nods, his eyes watching the blade now. He cannot stop this. He has to get through it, and keep them away from Anna.

"Where's the booze?" the second one demands.

"I don't have any. I give you money," Joseph answers.

"Cigarettes?"

"I don't smoke."

The big one delivers another quick blow to his head. Joseph puts his hands up to try to protect himself. Too late. His right eye is smarting and watering. It will be swollen shut within the hour.

"Don't lie to me, fucker," he says. "Where's the booze?"

"In the kitchen cupboard."

"That's better. Move." He uses his sneakered foot to prod Joseph towards the stairs.

Joseph shuffles in his slippers across the linoleum floor. The second teenager finds the light switch, snaps it on. Joseph's eyes sting at the harsh whiteness. Now he can see his assailants are young and that scares him. The young are stupid. Joseph feels panic clogging his throat, making it hard to breathe. He feels the back of his knees begin to tremble. The one with the knife is calm, lounging against the wall. He's tall and thin with black hair that's too long. A hunting knife. Joseph registers this; a hunting knife with a leather handle and a six-inch blade. It's shiny silver, a beautiful knife.

Joseph moves towards the pantry, swings open the door. He knows there is a bottle of wine, and maybe whisky somewhere in there. He stands looking at the neat jars of dill pickles that he and Anna preserved in the fall. I should have some of that pea soup, he's thinking. I have not had that for a while. I didn't know we had a can in here. His mind is absorbed in the task of listing what is in this cupboard. He's forgotten why he opened the door.

"Move." The tough one shoves him in the back. Joseph jerks back into the kitchen, and reaches behind the rice, finds the red wine.

"Not that shit," the kid says. "Get me some real booze, man. I'm getting tired of you."

Joseph reaches in again, and finds the bottle of Wiser's Whisky, its golden warmth winking at him as he draws it out into the light.

"Yeah," the kid grunts, grabbing the bottle, twisting off the cap.

Joseph does not want them in here, liquored up. He knows that is the worst danger he faces.

"I'll get you money, so you can go," Joseph offers.

"That's good," the kid with the knife says, taking the bottle from his partner, swigging long and hard, passing it back. "Get us money. And watches."

As Joseph turns towards the hallway, the kid grabs him by the back of the neck.

"I'm coming," he says, his arm almost companionable around Joseph's shoulders now, the whisky bottle swinging from his hand. "C'mon, Trip, it's time we took a tour here," he calls over his shoulder.

"There's nothing here," Joseph says too quickly. "I'll bring you what you need."

"Don't think so, pal," the one called Trip says. He moves in behind them, following down the hall, holding the knife loose and easy.

Joseph is taking deep breaths now, knowing he is leading them towards Anna. Half the bottle is gone, back and forth, guzzles of two and three ounces at a time disappearing down their throats. Joseph wants to slit their throats, feels it boil up inside him. He is clear-headed now; he'll take them to the front room, the parlour.

"Joseph," Ana's thin voice calls out.

Trip grabs Joseph, swings the knife up against his throat, suddenly as menacing as his partner.

"Tha' fuck?" he says, into Joseph's face. His breath, whisky and meanness, almost makes Joseph gag.

"He's a liar," the second kid says, and he moves down the hall, kicking open the partially closed bedroom door.

Anna turns her head, but she does not sit up. The moment she sees what her mind has already told her is happening, her bladder lets go. She can feel the warm trickle spreading between her legs. She lies still, watching as her husband Joseph is shoved through the door, the knife at his throat, his eye already puffed and swollen. He gives her a quick nod, to say everything is fine, Anna. She knows nothing will ever be fine again. The pool of warmth is collecting now near her hips, where her weight makes a slight indentation in the bed. She can smell it. It reminds her of Joey, changing his diaper. The sharp, ammonia smell of baby is so vivid she almost smiles.

"Get her jewelry," the shorter one orders. He's done enough of these B and E's to know old ladies have gold chains and bracelets and watches and earrings, all kinds of shit easy to dump at a pawnshop.

Joseph moves towards Anna's dresser. She can see he's dragging his leg slightly, but his hands are steady as he starts opening the drawers, looking for the box.

"Bottom," she says from the bed, never taking her eyes off the two men still drinking in her bedroom.

The one with the knife crosses the room and grabs the box out of Joseph's hands. Joseph watches him in the dresser mirror as he fumbles with the lid. The kid is right behind Joseph and Joseph imagines wheeling around and punching him fast and hard in the stomach, imagines cracking open his head. He remembers how to do this. He knew how to spar with the best of the them when he was younger. He could snap the kid in half. He could, once. But he is not young, and there is the other one. Joseph slumps into his old body, feeling old all the way to his bones for the first time. It is an oldness he will never again shake.

Trip finally opens the box and tinkling music now dances through the room. It is "The Blue Danube Waltz."

Anna is seeing her clean sheets snapping on the clothesline, in a spring breeze, in time to the music, all the urine washed away.

"Don't forget the rings, man," says the other one.

"Yeah," Trip grunts. "Gimme the ring." He's grabbing Joseph's hand, spotting the wide gold wedding band.

Joseph slips it off. He's worn it forty-eight years. It has never left his finger. He feels off balance as soon as it slides off, as though the whole weight of his body needs to shift to accommodate this change. He grips the side of the dresser.

"Hers too."

The tall one with the knife crosses to Anna and yanks the covers down to her waist. He presses the cold knife to her chest. Joseph, so old now, can no longer stand up. He slides down onto Anna's embroidered vanity stool, keeping his eyes on his wife. He opened the door. She told him not to answer it. He opened the door. That's all he can hear, going round inside his head, like an old record album with a warp.

*"Roby scho toby kazhut,"* he says to Anna.

"Quit talkin' that shit." The shorter one shoves him. The one with the knife stands over Anna.

"What did you say?" he demands.

"I said, do what they tell you," Joseph answers.

"That's good. That's right. Do what we say." Trip nods.

"I'll do it," Anna says, lifting her left hand, pulling on her wedding and engagement rings.

She's seeing her two babies. Anna had two miscarriages before her prayers were answered with Joey. Those first two babies flutter near her eyelids now. They do this from time to time. Even though she miscarried both times in her first trimester, they appear to Anna as fully formed children. She can see their white legs and dimpled elbows. She knows exactly what they look like, one boy, one girl, her little angels waiting for her in heaven.

"Hurry up," he says. "We ain't got all night, ya know."

"Hey man, you feel like doin' her?" the other one asks.

The knife presses harder, breaks skin, there is a thin line of red seeping through her nightgown.

"I dunno. Ya think?" Trip says, the whisky warm in his belly.

Anna is not clear what they mean, but she knows from the swaggering tone that it would be worse than what has happened so far. A deep sob wells up and out of her dry mouth. She's surprised the sound came from her. She struggles harder with the rings, pulling, but her fingers are full of arthritis these days; the rings will never come off. She needs to get some lotion from the bathroom. But she cannot get up, because then everyone will know that she wet her nightgown, in her bed. This puddle of shame must stay hidden. It's all her fault. And now they will kill her and Joseph.

Trip grabs her hand, yanks so hard it feels like her shoulder pops from its socket.

"Gimme those rings or I'll cut your finger off," he says calmly, the knife moving from her chest to her wrist. He is so casual, the blood in Joseph's veins freezes, then heats and pounds.

"Joseph," Anna says, her voice clear now across the room, carrying no hint of the pain searing along her arm, "please get me the lilac lotion from the bathroom cabinet. And then I will be able to give you the rings." She speaks directly to Trip.

"Go with him," Trip orders the other. Joseph realizes for the first time the man called Trip is in charge. He had thought it was the other way around, but he sees now this is exactly like in the railyard, where he worked for thirty-seven years. The ones to watch out for were the quiet, easy ones that did not raise their voices. He knows how bullies work. How can it help him now, an old man, in his slippers, shuffling down the hall, one eye swollen shut, his wife alone with a man who will kill her for no reason? How does this knowing help him? How?

He finds the lotion.

When he gets back to the room he sees Anna is talking to Trip in a low, soothing voice. She's explaining about the jewelry, how much he can get for each piece.

"That one is eighteen carats. Don't let them cheat you," she's advising. The need to survive at any cost has taken over now. It is going to be okay. She should get this soiled mattress outside, but who will help her move it? This is her only concern now, this bed, the state it is in.

The second man throws the lotion to her. As it's bouncing on the bed, he drops the empty whisky bottle on the maple floor. Joseph cringes as though hit. Anna is trying to stretch her aching arm, so that she can grab the lotion. Her fingers find the bottle, squeeze.

"I give you two minutes," Trip says. "Then I'm cutting the fucking finger off."

She works the lotion under the ring, twisting the bands round and round her gnarly knuckles. Anna has always loved the colour and the smell of lilacs. It's what she uses in her bath, dabs behind her ears and on the inside of her wrists. Lilac water. But right now, Anna is gagging back bile in her throat as she rubs and rubs and twists. She will never use lilac water again to scent her skin, and in May she will close all her windows, choking on the smell of fresh lilacs.

The rings come free, slide easily off her finger. Just like that, the lotion works.

Trip puts them in his pocket, nods.

"Money and car keys," Trip orders Joseph, moving back to where he is sitting, slumped on the stool at the dresser, putting the knife now at Joseph's back. "Move."

Anna listens to them going back down the hallway. It's almost over. How long has this gone on? She has no idea. She does not move. She barely breathes.

"That it, man?" The second one prods Joseph. "You lyin' again?" He gives Joseph a shove.

Joseph has one credit card and $34 in his wallet. He takes the $40 of grocery money out of the coffee cup on the second shelf above the stove. He hands over his car keys. He is so tired now, he no longer even feels frightened.

"That's all," Joseph says. Waits.

"Let's get the car and get out of here," Trip orders. He reaches over and cuts the phone cord in the kitchen with his knife. They move to the door.

"So long," Trip says. And they are gone.

Joseph slips quietly to the floor, winded.

Anna hears their car start in the driveway. The air in the house is so thick, she finds it hard to breathe. She swings her old legs out of the bed, hugging her injured arm to her body like a broken wing, using her other hand to grope her way along the walls, down the hall, to the kitchen.

"Get up," she says to Joseph, when she finds him sitting on the floor, his head leaning against the rose wallpaper.

He looks up at her through his one eye, the other swollen shut.

"Get up," she says again, stronger this time. "I need help changing the sheets and the mattress. I need to take a bath. Joseph, I need you to help me. I can't do it with my arm."

Joseph stumbles to his feet. Anna stretches her good hand to him, and he takes it. Anna stops at the hallway closet to get fresh linen. She finds her bucket, and scrub cloth. She strips the bed first and scrubs and scrubs the spot where she was leaking. She goes to her kitchen pantry and mechanically finds the box of baking soda. Anna sprinkles soda on the bed, scrubbing hard. She wants to turn the mattress over. She and Joseph struggle, grunting, heaving, but they simply cannot manage it.

She covers the damp mattress with clean sheets and new blankets. She should let it dry first, but she cannot. Anna wants to hide the naked spot on the mattress. Even with new bedding her eyes are drawn there like a magnet.

Joseph helps Anna remove her nightgown, and get into the bathtub. She scrubs her paper-thin skin as thoroughly as she scoured the bed. Joseph sits on the kitchen chair, almost napping, but his mind jumps at the last second. Just as he's about to ease over the edge into sleep, he jerks, his heart hammering. This will become normal for Joseph, sleep stolen from him at the last second. This will be his new pattern.

Anna calls to him when she is out of the bath. She has them dress in their good Sunday clothes, right down to their underwear. The police will be coming, and so it's important. She gets one of Joseph's good woolen socks from his dresser, one that's never been darned, and fills it with ice, pressing it against his battered eye.

They sit on their wooden chairs in the kitchen until the sun comes up, until the neighbourhood starts waking up, until they hear car doors slamming, a child's high-pitched yell, because it would be rude to go next door in the middle of the night, disturbing people.

When the neighbourhood is awake, Anna and Joseph shuffle side by side down their driveway. Anna's arm is in the sling she has fashioned from a good silk scarf, the one her son Joey brought her last Mother's Day.

The Walker comes down her path, across the street, just as Mr. and Mrs. Warbanski reach the end of their empty driveway. Joseph looks directly at her, fiercely, with his one good eye, staring into her face across the paved street. He makes three quick signs of the cross. The intensity of that look is a like a slap to her.

The Walker turns left, not right. And for the first time anyone can remember, she walks counter-clockwise, loop after loop after loop, head down.

# Chapter 9

Sandra McMaster has been in Winnipeg for two days, covering a political convention, and she is bored. She is sitting in her hotel room taking a break and having a cigarette, because there's no smoking allowed inside the convention room and she's sick and tired of puffing outside on the street.

Sandra McMaster is a syndicated columnist. Her stories are printed in two national newspapers, eight Canadian daily papers and several weeklies, all owned by the same man. The policies the delegates are talking about at this convention are humdrum. Good background for her to have in her head, but she'll be lucky to get any kind of story out of it.

She flips on the TV. The local newscast leads with a report about a home invasion. The victims, an elderly couple, were not seriously hurt, and nothing was stolen except their Buick. But what catches Sandra's interest, what makes her sit up straight on the bed is this tidbit near the end of the report: "...Police have not ruled out a connection between this invasion and the killing of four dogs in the same neighbourhood several weeks ago, but say it is unlikely. The dogs were poisoned with strychnine-laced hamburger meat. A police spokesperson says the home invasion victims did not own a dog. Police are now looking for two teenage males..."

"Now there's a story," Sandra says, getting off the bed, grabbing the keys to her rented car. She is going in search of Oakwood.

She finds Glendale Avenue easily, using the map the front desk clerk has given her. When Sandra arrives in Oakwood, she parks at the old-fashioned gas station with two pumps, and crosses the boulevard.

It's mid-morning, and Glendale Avenue seems almost eerily quiet to her. Sandra's heels click against the silent Saturday as she walks briskly towards the only person on the street. She frowns. The woman coming towards her is wearing a yellow rain jacket, but there is not a cloud in the sky.

"Excuse me," Sandra calls as soon as she's within earshot.

The woman does not even look up. She's walking intently, staring down.

"Hello?" Sandra tries again. "I was hoping you could help me out." The woman still does not look up. Maybe she's deaf, Sandra thinks. Great.

Sandra walks down Glendale Avenue with her notebook, observing the tidy yards, the modest homes, a child's tricycle, a sprinkler swooshing. At several houses people look out, but when they see her they move away from their windows.

Sandra goes up to a house, rings the doorbell. No answer. She is persistent. Watching from her kitchen window, Janice sighs, wipes her soapy hands on the tea towel, goes out the front door and down the walk. At least it's not television; her hair is a mess.

"Can I help you?" she calls out to Sandra.

Sandra is two doors away, but she quickly crosses over to Janice and introduces herself, looking her straight in the eye.

"I was beginning to think no one actually lives in Oakwood," she says.

"I think we are all a bit shell-shocked," Janice answers. "It's been a hard few weeks here. The Warbanskis are sweet people. That is why you are here, I imagine?"

"Yes. Do they have children, grandchildren?" Sandra asks.

"One son, Joey. He never married. No grandkids."

"How long have they lived here?" Sandra is scribbling on her notepad, but she maintains eye contact with her interview subject. She has learned how to jot down key points while keeping a conversation going.

"Forever. More than forty years." Janice looks away, towards the Warbanskis' house. There is already a For Sale sign on the lawn of the next house. The Bolton family, owners of Fifi, plan to leave Oakwood for good.

Janice goes on. "Anna told me how Joseph came to work on her father's farm, for the harvest." Sandra McMaster says nothing; she just waits. "Joseph had no family. They got trapped behind the wrong lines during World War II. He never talks about it. The war, I mean. Anna says he had a strong back. That's what caught her fancy, his strong back."

Sandra is writing. Finally, she asks about the dog connection.

"No. They didn't have a dog." Janice frowns.

"Police are investigating possible connections. Between the dog killings and the Warbanski incident," Sandra tells her.

"That's funny," Janice says. "The police told us they were pretty sure the dog murders had to be an inside job. I mean, someone who lives nearby, who maybe got tired of them. "

"Think about it, though," Sandra says. "It's a lot easier to rob a house if there are no dogs barking, isn't it?"

"Oh." Janice covers her mouth with her hand.

"What is it?"

"The dog next door to the Warbanskis was killed. The poodle, Fifi. She did bark a lot, whenever a stranger came up their path." Janice is thinking out loud. She shudders. "It could be, I guess."

"Thank you," Sandra says. She makes small talk about the flowers, shakes Janice's hand, crosses the boulevard. She is sitting in her rented car, adding to her notes when she looks up. Along the brick wall of the garage there's black, scrawled graffiti. She gets back out of her car.

"Yeah, I'm the owner." The pocket on his grease-spotted overalls says Walt. He's in the front office of the garage.

"Tell me about the graffiti," she says.

"It's summer. Kids are always going around in summer with their spray cans, tagging."

"Does it bother you?" she asks.

"Costs me money to keep painting over it, yeah," he says.

"Can you make out what it says, what it means?" she asks. "Can you come out and take a look?"

Walt obliges her.

"That's just garbage," he points to some of the graffiti. "This here—" He moves closer. "—Those are the initials of a local gang. "

"What kind of gang?" She is scribbling.

"Teenagers. You know, punks."

"Are they a big problem here?" she asks.

"Seems to be getting worse," Walt says. "Windows in my garage were smashed about a month ago."

"Thank you," Sandra says.

She gets into her car, heads downtown, and parks in the underground garage at the hotel. She takes the elevator to her room, turns on her laptop, retrieves her contact list and finds the phone number of her favourite criminologist, who is a professor in Toronto.

There is a new study on youth gangs just being released in the United States, he tells her. The conclusions suggest youth gangs are becoming much more systematic, actually targeting neighbourhoods and then over a period of several months moving in, escalating their activities. It is a patient, step-by-step approach to scare away residents and control territory. This study was conducted in three mid-sized American cities. He listens to Sandra describe the graffiti, smashed windows, dead dogs, and home invasion.

"Based on what you are telling me," he says, "Oakwood sounds like the classic test case. I think this is a wake-up call for all Canadian cities. These kids are organized."

Sandra McMaster writes her column about Oakwood, the community targeted by a sophisticated youth gang. It is picked up by the wire service and printed in subscriber papers across the country. Pay attention to the graffiti, it says, that's the first sign of what is going on in your neighbourhood.

Phoebe has been studying the graffiti in her neighbourhood, and she copies some of it down in the notebook that is now her journal. What she copies is also scrawled across the gas station wall, the same garage but near the bushes at the back lane, where the reporter did not go.

*Dance to the tension of a world on the edge,* she copies. She writes this over and over, printing it, writing backhand, forming tall square letters and round, squat ones. She writes until one whole page in her diary is filled.

Phoebe likes the way the words roll from her tongue. Dance to the tension of a world on the edge, she whispers to herself as she's falling asleep.

—

Joey Warbanski sits in his renovated Euro-kitchen. It is Saturday morning, and he's reading Sandra McMaster's column about Oakwood. It gives him a chill up his spine. He grew up on those streets, riding his bike, necking at the far end of the beach where the rocks cast deep shadows, drinking apple cider in the graveyard and smoking the occasional joint, as almost all the fifteen-year-olds in Oakwood did back then. Joey folds the newspaper carefully and puts it into the recycling box. He is supposed to be teaching summer school right now to earn extra money for his trip to Australia and New Zealand next year. Joey works hard and enjoys teaching high school geography, but his real love is traveling, and every second year he takes off on a three-month journey.

This summer is turning out different than planned. He dropped his summer session and his parents are living with him now. Joseph says he and Anna will not go back to the house on Glendale Avenue. Might as well try to sell it, he tells Joey. Won't get much for it, he never even cleaned out the eaves this year. Well, he won't be doing that now. Maybe Joey could just go check on the tomatoes out back.

Joey looks up. His father is in the kitchen doorway. "How are you feeling this morning?" he asks him.

"Fine," Joseph answers. "Can't complain." It's been two days, and Joseph's eye is cracking open again. It sits in its swollen pouch, eggplant purple.

Joey stirs his coffee. He had been buttering his toast, rushing to get ready for work when he got the phone call from his parents' neighbour. It had been an ordinary, bright summer morning. Then he picked up the phone. It stopped him dead in his tracks, the image of his parents being held at knifepoint. Everything has slowed down since then. Now the seconds seem to tick by individually in Joey's head. He finds himself staring out of the window for long stretches, not seeing anything.

Joey knows he should have made his mother and father move out of Oakwood, after the dogs. He should have made them come home with him right then. He is an only child, and his guilt for not properly protecting his parents is what beats through him, over and over.

His father sits down at the table.

"Is Mom awake yet?" Joey asks. His parents are sleeping in his bedroom, although his mother protested about displacing him. Joey is sleeping on his folding cot in the cool basement; his back and neck are full of cricks when he wakes up now.

"I'm here," Anna says, joining them in the kitchen. She automatically crosses the room and puts an affectionate hand on Joey's shoulder.

"Did you get the pamphlets?" Joseph asks.

"Yes. Hang on, I'll get them," Joey jumps up, goes to his living room where a growing pile of papers collects on his coffee table.

"I really think you are going to like one of these," he says, coming back into the kitchen. "I had no idea there were so many to choose from."

Joey reaches for the coffeepot for a refill.

"Let me," his mother says. She hovers in back of the men, near the fridge and stove. She brings coffee and milk to the table.

"There are fresh bagels and cream cheese, " Joey says.

"Oh," Anna says politely. "We'll eat in a few minutes. No rush." Anna will make their usual breakfast: porridge. Joseph will not eat bagels, she knows.

Anna joins the men at the table, pulling a brochure towards her.

"Look," she says.

His mother is pointing at the crisp photos of houses nestled around a man-made pond inside a gated community.

"I was looking at these brochures last night," Joey says. He was home by seven o'clock, because he won't leave his parents alone after dark, but they were already in his bed. The doctor at the hospital who examined the Warbanskis prescribed pills. Anti-anxiety; the pills are supposed to make them drowsy. Joseph and Anna swallow these pills after supper and lie down, waiting for the drugs to put them to sleep. Joseph waits and waits, but it does no good.

"I can take you to see some of these, if you want. If you're up to it." Joey says.

"I want to see them," Anna says. "Look how everything is new." She's flipping inside the brochure, to the shiny bathroom faucets and electric garage door opener.

"This one," Joseph says. "Let's go here." He passes Joey a pamphlet. A Full Service Community, it says. Each unit has a view of the artificial lake. These houses are bungalow style, so there are no stairs to navigate. Row after row of gleaming tri-pane windows, salmon stucco and brass doorknobs stare up at Joey.

"Yes, Joseph, I like it." Anna is almost excited.

"Well, okay. Let's go check it out," Joey says. "We could go now."

"I'll just make breakfast for your father, dear," Anna gets to her feet.

"Sure," Joey says. "I'm going to mow the lawn. We'll go in an hour."

It is mid-morning when Joey and his parents go out into the sunshine. Joey insists his father wear a pair of his sunglasses, to protect his eye. Bending to get into his little red Mustang, Joey glances over and his mouth tugs upwards. His father looks almost snazzy, sitting in the low-slung bucket seat wearing his fedora and Joey's shades.

It takes half an hour to drive to the newly created community of Four Winds. The Warbanskis pass six or seven other new developments, some fenced and some gated, mushrooming in the prairie soil, just outside the reach of the city.

"This is it," Joey says, turning off the highway.

"It looks nice," his mother says. Along both sides of the access road, crushed white rocks surround juniper bushes. From here it is impossible to see the houses which are tucked behind a stone wall.

Joey stops his car at the cross arms, which look exactly like a railway intersection. An uniformed security guard opens the door of his brick booth, ducks under the barricade, and approaches Joey's side of the car.

Joey rolls down his window.

"Hi. My parents are interested in seeing one of these homes," he says.

"Do you have an appointment?" the guard asks.

"No," Joey says, brow furrowing.

"I can't let you in without an appointment," the guard says.

"An appointment with whom?" Joey asks.

"There is a licensed realtor. Or the management company that operates Four Winds," the guard says. "I can get you a brochure."

"That's okay, I have the brochure."

"Have a nice day then." The guard straightens away from the car.

"Wait," Joey says. "We've driven all the way out here and my parents really wanted to see this place. Can I make an appointment right now? Do you have a phone?"

The guard considers.

"Do you have any identification?" he asks finally.

"Yes." Joey is reaching for his wallet, handing over his license. "I'm a teacher. Full time. Ten years at the same school division," he adds quickly.

"Hang on," the guard says, taking the license, heading towards his booth. They can see him picking up the phone through the Plexiglas.

"I like it here," Joseph says.

"I do, too," Anna agrees.

The guard is walking back towards them, a clipboard under his arm.

"Okay," he says. "Mr. Peterson will see you. Sign here." He's handing Joey back his license, sliding the clipboard through the open window.

"Thank you," Joey says. "Who is Mr. Peterson?"

"He's the property manager. His office is just inside, to your left. "

Joey is writing his name on the clipboard, in the first column. The second column requests his license number, which the security guard has already filled in. The third column asks him to print the name of whom he is visiting, and the time of his arrival.

"Can I see inside your booth?" Joseph asks, leaning over to talk to the security guard.

"Sorry, sir. Only authorized personnel are allowed in there. But Mr. Peterson will go over our security highlights with you."

The guard goes back to his booth, pushes a button and the arms to Four Winds open to them.

Joey turns left. He feels strangely exposed in here. There are no trees, only a few spindly twigs budding along the road. A man in an Italian suit is standing outside his office, waiting for them.

"Mr. Warbanski," the man says, coming forward with hand outstretched first to Joseph, then Joey, and then Anna. "Welcome to our community. Would you care for some coffee or tea?" He's leading them inside to his office, which has a couch, coffee table and armchairs in addition to a desk and computer station.

"I'd like coffee," Joey says.

"We've already had our cup," Anna says, answering for her and Joseph. Joseph takes off the sunglasses, sliding them into his jacket pocket. Mr. Peterson notes the black eye and files the information for later.

"Please, sit down. Now, how can I help you?" he asks, once they are settled and Joey has a fresh cup of coffee.

"My parents would like to see one of your homes. One of the units with two bedrooms." Joey says.

"Certainly we can take you through a few of our model homes." Mr. Peterson is nodding. "We only have a few bungalows left. They are selling faster than projected. Now, for a real sense of this place, its unique character, I'd also like to take you to our lake and community park, and of course there are the miles of paved jogging...well, in your case," a quick and charming smile to Anna as he corrects himself, "walking trails."

"Wait," Joseph says, as Mr. Peterson draws a breath to continue.

"Yes?" he says.

"Is that a camera?" he asks, pointing upwards to a video camera tucked into the right hand corner of the ceiling. It is pointing at them.

"Yes," Mr. Peterson says. "There's no reason for alarm. That's just Ron watching us. He's the security guard you met at the front gate," he adds.

"Where else do you have cameras?" Joseph wants to know.

"Well, our security is state of the art. We are setting the standard that other communities will be imitating." Mr. Peterson shifts gears; this usually comes near the end of his talk with potential clients, after the tour. Now he knows what the black eye means, how to incorporate it. "We have sixteen cameras operating at all times in the public areas of our community." He smiles. "You might have noticed one recording your license plates when you drove through the gate. No? Good. I'm not going to tell you exactly where it is because that would defeat the purpose, wouldn't it? And each of our units has a camera attached to the back deck, so we can see individual backyards." He looks directly at Joseph. "No one can prowl around your yard without us knowing about it," he says. "We have a security guard on duty twenty-four hours a day, seven days a week. He monitors the screens. Another staff member also has access to a bank of screens. Of course, you already know we only allow people inside who have appointments, and that includes your guests. We require that you tell us about all visitors. We also do patrols at night. We've never had a break-in or a theft here. But each home is fully alarmed, just in case. You can never be too careful."

"I see," says Joseph.

"Well." Joey coughs. "Maybe you can tell us a bit more about the house, the price. The fees for all this."

Joseph raises his hand, cutting off his son. He leans forward in his chair.

"What would happen here if somebody was walking round and round?" he asks. His one good eye is staring at Mr. Peterson intently.

"I'm sorry?" The property manager is not sure what he is talking about, but he knows it will be the deal breaker.

"Would you allow somebody to walk around and around in circles?" Joseph says again.

Mr. Peterson picks his way carefully through this minefield.

"I can't say it's something we've encountered here in our community in the two years we've existed," he starts.

"But would you allow it?" Joseph is getting agitated. His hand clenches the arm of the chair.

"Joseph," his wife says softly.

"I think you've brought up a very important point, Mr. Warbanski," Mr. Peterson says. He's back on solid ground. "It's not me who allows these things. The residents make all decisions," he says, with that direct gaze again. "The residents have meetings, and you create the by-laws. You decide what is allowed, and what is not allowed inside these gates. Then you vote."

"How would the residents vote?" Joseph insists, still tense.

"On someone walking in circles?" Mr. Peterson is careful again. "I can't speak for the residents," he says, "but if I was a betting man, I would think that would not be allowed inside Four Winds."

"Okay," Joseph says, sitting back. His fingers uncurl.

Mr. Peterson knows he has gambled correctly. He smiles warmly at Joey. "More coffee?" he offers.

"Dad, should we go take a look now?" Joey asks.

"That's not necessary," Joseph says.

"What?" Joey says.

Joseph ignores his son. He looks only at Anna, turning his body to face her fully, as though it is only the two of them in the room.

She is sitting in her armchair, her fingers twisting round and round where her wedding band used to be. It feels like it's still there, like a phantom leg.

"*Holubenko?*" Joseph asks.

Little dove. Joey's eyes sting. He has to clear his throat and turn away. He has not heard his father call his mother that since he was a boy, and never publicly like this, in front of an absolute stranger.

"Yes," she says.

"Bring me the papers. We'll take it," Joseph says.

"Dad. Wait. How much is this, anyway?" he says to Mr. Peterson, rushing now to protect his mother and father.

"It doesn't matter about the money," Joseph says to his son. "Bring me the papers," he repeats.

He signs. His dove, his Anna is safe now. The purchase allows for immediate occupancy. Mr. and Mrs. Warbanski buy the second house they have ever owned, sight unseen.

By the time they are back in Joey's car, heading down the highway, thick clouds are rolling across the sky. The sudden summer storm picks up dust in the open fields and swirls it onto the roads. Fat raindrops begin to splatter down just as they pull into Joey's driveway.

A car is parked in front of Joey's house. A man gets out and approaches the Warbanskis as they struggle up the walk, against the wind.

"Excuse me? Joseph Warbanski?" he calls through the wind.

Joey turns quickly, blocking his parents.

"What do you want?" He has to speak louder than normal, over the rolling thunder.

"I'm Philip Janzen, reporter with the *Free Press*. I'd like a few minutes to talk with you. Please."

"No," says Joey.

"No," says Joseph.

"It's raining," Anna says. "He's getting wet." Her look rebukes Joey for his bad manners.

"They caught the guys," Philip tells them. "That's why I'm here."

Joey sighs. "I need to get them out of the rain." He turns, urging his parents forward, up the walk. "Just for a minute," he adds.

The reporter follows them inside.

"I'll make you some coffee," Anna says, going towards the kitchen. Joseph follows her and then stays in the kitchen. He won't come into the living room while the reporter is there. Joey carries the tray of cups and biscuits his mother has prepared, because she still cannot lift anything properly with her arm. She tells the boy Philip about her arm, and her husband's eye. She's doing the exercises the doctor showed her for her shoulder and elbow, and Joseph puts ice packs on his face. They are both fine now, she tells him.

"Tell me about the guys." Joey says finally. "Mom, are you sure you want to hear this?"

"Yes," she says.

In the kitchen, Joseph moves closer to the door so he can hear.

"One of them is sixteen. Police can't release his name because he's a young offender. It's not his first offense," Philip says. "He drifts around, used to be in a group home. The second guy was stupid. "

"Trip," Anna says. "He didn't seem stupid."

"That's one of his nicknames," Philip says. "He's nineteen, goes by a few names. He's also done time, for break and enter, and assault with a weapon. Car theft. They caught him because he was actually trying to pawn your wedding rings, even though they are engraved and easy to trace. Stupid."

"They have our rings back?" Anna says. "Oh. My rings."

"The rings are safe, but of course police need them as evidence. You'll get them once the case is over, I imagine." Philip says. "And your car has been picked up just south of the city. There's some damage, but it's not a write-off."

"We don't want the car," Joseph says, from the kitchen doorway. "You tell them that." He's speaking to Philip. "You tell them to keep it." He goes back into the kitchen.

"Did the police say why they did this? What did they say?" Joey wants to know.

"No particular reason. Looking for money, or kicks. The usual," says Philip. Anna leans back in her chair. It is quiet in the room. They can hear the steady beat of the rain.

"And the dogs? What about those dogs? Fifi?" she asks finally.

"The dogs. Seems a few people jumped the gun on that one," Philip says. "Police say there's no connection. The sixteen-year-old has an airtight alibi: he was in lock-up that day. The other one, Trip, has witnesses who say he was at a friend's. And the 7-11 video camera has him on tape buying cigarettes right near her apartment around the time they figure those dogs got poisoned. No connection," Philip repeats, shrugging his shoulders.

That's what the media will report now. But the residents of Glendale Avenue will always say, in one breath, when the dogs died and the Warbanskis were invaded. Phoebe's little brothers grow up believing these things happened on the same night, the two events flattening into one snapshot. Just the way that Toronto reporter wrote it, Sandra, the one who was here in her silk blouse. It's more like she said, to the people of Oakwood. Connected.

"Police say they doubt they'll ever catch that dog-killer," Philip adds. "The cops..." He glances at Anna. "...sorry, the police told me that after forty-eight hours they don't even try. It's a waiting game now. They have to wait and see if someone cracks. That's the way these ones get solved—someone walks in out of the blue and confesses. Or not."

"Well," Anna says. She gets to her feet, starts moving across the room. "Thank you."

"I wanted to ask you a few questions about how you feel now that these two have been arrested," Philip says quickly.

"I must go check on my husband," Anna says, and goes into the kitchen.

Philip sighs. He knew it was a long shot, that he would likely not get that interview. He pulls out his notepad, flips it open.

"So what do you think should be done with these guys?" Philip asks Joey instead.

"Lock them up. Throw away the key," he says. Then he feels a quick bolt of fear as he watches the reporter write that down. Joey is in the phone book. Anyone can find his house. They could come here, or their friends could come looking for him.

"Wait. Scratch that. Here is a statement on behalf of my parents and me." He clears his throat. "We hope these boys, these young men, get the counseling and help that they need," Joey says.

"That's a lie," Philip says. "You don't believe that."

"The truth," Joey says, "is that I don't know what I believe anymore. Print that."

Philip frowns, and he does not print that. Too wishy-washy, it doesn't go anywhere. Instead, his article on the Sunday Life page focuses on Joey's care for his parents, the generosity of the school in giving him more than a week off with pay, and how well Joseph and Anna Warbanski are recuperating. It mentions the sleeping pills, which Philip found lined up in the bathroom when he went to use the john. This part Joey cuts out of the Sunday paper before his parents see it, saying there was a coupon he had to have on the other side. His mother, Joey knows, would be humiliated for people to read that she's taking pills to cope. The article also includes an interview with the superintendent of the Riverpark School Division, who is handling the money pouring in from complete strangers. No one is sure why people are sending money. Maybe it makes them feel they are fixing something. Joseph Warbanski does not need it. He has a good pension from the railway, indexed to inflation for the rest of his life, and a wisely chosen portfolio of blue chip stocks performing so well the interest is being gobbled up in taxes. He is thinking of going back to a regular savings account at the credit union.

Anna and Joseph like the newspaper article with a hole in it when they see it, carefully reading it line by line out loud in Joey's kitchen.

"You are a good son," Anna tells Joey. "I'm glad the newspaper prints that."

—

The oak trees turn their backs to the rain, spines curving, shoulders hunching against the wind. Their leaves turn inside out so that everything in the graveyard is olive, bent, and shaking.

Jill is huddling inside The Nest.

One of the rules used to be that she and Phoebe could only come here together. Now Jill comes here alone, especially on this kind of Saturday. Before Phoebe left for that sissy camp she pulled her blanket and her comics out of The Nest and took them home.

Jill is watching how the river snakes silver through the pounding rain, twisting and dodging the heavy drops. She is quite sure that if she could travel far enough, on this snake's back, she would come to the spot where its head emerges, where its sharp eyes and fangs snap at the land, trying to crawl ashore. Jill would like to go there.

Right now she squeezes through the bushes, out of The Nest, into the rain. She left her bike at home, so she walks through the puddles in her boots. Her windbreaker is plastered to her thin frame and her hair is matted down. Jill is whistling under her breath. She figures she'll go listen to The Witch. This is the kind of day she usually plays.

Jill lifts her face to the rain. It's slanting to the left, so that means the dining room window will be propped open. The Witch likes to open her windows when it rains. She's always ready for a day exactly like this, waiting in her yellow jacket. Jill and Phoebe knew all these facts; it was in their book.

Jill comes at the house from the back, crawls under the hole in the fence and works her way to the dining room window. She can hear the piano already. This side of the house is overgrown with raspberry bushes; it's time to sneak over here with her lunch box and pick the juicy berries until her fingers are stained red. The bushes are scratchy, and Jill tries to avoid touching them as she makes her way along the side of the house. She puts her hands against the wood siding instead, for balance, inching her way along, occasionally picking a wet, bright raspberry as she goes. Good, it's loud here.

Jill wants to be out of the house today because He is over, Mr. Findley, with his round, pink cheeks and his laugh that is always too loud. Jill hates him because he pats her and Delores on the head, like they are dogs, and he always calls Delores Lois, as if there's something wrong with her real name, or maybe he can't remember it. If Phoebe were here, she'd make fun of him with Jill and they would laugh at his big nose. Mr. Findley is one of her mother's bosses. He comes over about once a month on Saturday afternoons and always pretends he is very interested in Bea's fashion designs, but Jill knows it's only pretending because of the way his eye ticks. Then Bea and Mr. Findley disappear into the bedroom with the door closed, and they cannot be disturbed. Or else. He puts Sally in the closet. He says he can't stand Sally, she gives him the creeps since she moved into the bedroom. Afterwards, he takes Bea grocery shopping because Bea does not have a car, and he lets Delores and Jill buy anything they want in the store, at least food stuff, not toys. Jill goes for fudge cookies. And then he leaves. He never stays for supper, even though the fridge is full. On these kinds of Saturdays, Jill stands in front of that bursting fridge, looking at the different things she can eat. All she has to do is reach in and grab something, but all those choices make her tired, and so she doesn't bother with any of it. Delores eats and hides whatever she can.

Jill sits under the dining room window, under the eaves where it's dry, and listens to The Witch play Bach. Each note seems to tumble out of the window and pearl with the raindrops on the leaves. Phoebe thinks this piano music stuff is boring, and her mother does not like her out in the rain, so Jill has been making this trip on her own since spring. She doesn't care. She leans her head back against the house and closes her eyes, squatting between the raspberry bushes.

When the notes start crashing together, bunching themselves into knots, Jill's eyes fly open. In the mounds of wet, black earth she sees the worms have come to the surface. She reaches out and grabs for one quickly, but it slithers and disappears beneath the earth. Jill leans forward, onto her knees. She reaches into the earth, which is wet on top but warm underneath. And now she's digging with both hands, tunneling down, down, down. She wants to see where the worms go, how they go so quickly. She's tugging at the earth in time to the tangled music. She wants to be as skinny and long as a worm so she can slide under it all. Suddenly, it stops. The piano stops.

Jill stares at the earth. She's muddy up to her elbows. She sits back on her heels. She's tired. She wishes she had enough energy to tunnel down into this house, where she could live in her basement. Jill wants to be like The Witch; alone, waiting for rain, not talking to anyone.

This is how Margaret Sutherland, standing in her dining room window, sees her. Margaret shakes her head, and draws her drapes closed.

# CHAPTER 10

Laurel can't settle down. The three kids are in bed, Brian is watching TV, and Laurel wants to crawl out of her skin. It's another muggy night. The fan is whirring in the kitchen, lifting the hair off her face and neck. She opens the window, then closes the window, stoops to pick up bread crusts under the baby's high chair, wipes a spot of juice from the counter. She cannot take it.

She paces to the family room, a jumble of toys and pillows and mess and Brian.

"I'm going for a walk," she says.

"Now?" He looks up from the TV screen.

"I won't go far," she says.

Since the Warbanskis were robbed, Brian does not trust the night. He does not sit outside on the steps anymore. He found himself in Wal-Mart, buying a wooden baseball bat, which he now keeps under the bed. Laurel reached down there looking for her slippers a couple of mornings ago, and pulled out the bat instead.

"What's this?" she asked him.

Brian was sitting on his side of the bed, pulling on his socks. He didn't want her to know he is worrying. He didn't want to scare himself by saying out loud why he has this wooden bat.

"Baseball," he said. "I thought I'd teach Jamie the basics." He concentrated on buttoning up his shirt.

"Oh," Laurel said. "Why is it in here?"

"It's a surprise."

She frowned.

"When are you giving it to him?"

"What's with the third degree?" He started feeling defensive. He knew he was digging himself into a hole here.

"You don't normally come home with toys and then hide them, that's all," she said tartly. "It's not his birthday or anything."

"Maybe I do now," he said. "You're not the only one who's allowed, you know."

"Allowed what, exactly?" Laurel was on her feet, hands on her hips.

"Allowed to take off across the country. Allowed to hide things under the bed. You know what I'm talking about." Brian yanked on his pants, striding towards the dresser.

The fight went out of Laurel.

"He's only four, Brian," she said in a quieter voice. "Maybe you should start with one of those plastic bats and those nerf balls. That's all I'm saying."

He turned to face her.

"Okay," he said. Laurel did not often concede a fight. He knew enough to get out of this one while he could. "I'll keep this bat for me, maybe give it to him in a few years. I'll stop at Wal-Mart on my way home from work and get a plastic set for Jamie."

"Good," Laurel said then, sliding the wooden bat back under the bed. Brian knotted his tie.

Now she is standing there with her hands on her hips again, and Brian turns down the volume on the TV.

"Just going to stroll around Oakwood, are you?" he says.

"I'm not going to act like a prisoner. This is like a cage," she says, tugging at her white blouse, holding it away from her skin to get some breathing room.

"Go then," he says, like he doesn't care. But he'll watch from the window to make sure she is safe.

"I am." She's turning on her heel, twisting the deadbolt on the front door, and stepping out into the heavy air.

Laurel does not walk around Oakwood. She goes directly across Glendale Avenue, to the beach. It's so quiet she can hear the moths beating their wings against the street lamp overhead.

Laurel goes to the swings, immediately liking the feel of the cool chain links under her palms. She pushes herself with her feet to get started, then she's bending her knees, pumping and going higher. The breeze this creates against her face and arms and legs is exactly what she needed and she's smiling.

Laurel is soaring now. She's swinging against the black sky, white cotton blouse flattening and billowing as though it's breathing. When she's at the highest point in the arc she thinks about jumping into the night. Because she could fly—that's how it feels tonight with the air so thick it would hold her up—if she just let go.

She remembers something from being a child and leans back. Yes, this is the game. You swing with your head all the way back. So now her house across the street is upside down, a whizzing blur, Gary's attic next door is really a basement, the breeze against her exposed throat tickles and her hair is brushing the sand. Her arms strain with leaning backwards. Go backwards upside down or jump into the night? She is suspended on this swing trying to think, trying to decide when upside-down feet move into her view. A man's feet.

The blood rushes to her head as she sits up quickly, feeling dizzy. The swing is slowing.

"Laurel." The voice is low.

She twists the swing around.

"Brian, you surprised me."

Brian leans against the pole that holds up the swing set. At this angle he can see both Laurel and the front door of his house. He won't take his eyes off the front door, just in case.

"So," he says.

"So," she says, scuffing her feet in the sand, quiet now, heartbeat slowing, her hair settling heavily onto her nape once again.

"I asked for a transfer to Halifax. I found out today it's a go. It's a promotion, into management."

She looks up.

"The ocean," she says. "The other ocean."

"Yeah."

"So the kids would be able to swim in the ocean," she repeats.

"Yeah."

"It's time to leave here," she says.

"It's time, Laurel."

"Okay." Laurel gets off the swing, and goes to him. She puts her arms around his neck and leans into his chest, holding on. Brain rests his chin on the top of her head, still watching his house.

"I know what happened, Laurel," he says quietly. "I know all about it."

"Oh," she says, rubbing her cheek against the denim of his shirt. Neither one of them will mention this again. Now three houses are up for sale on Glendale Avenue. The Boltons' house, the Warbanskis', and the Murrays'.

Laurel thinks they are going this time because Brian knows about Gary, about the attic. Brian believes he's taking Laurel away because his wife, the mother of his three children, poisoned the dogs of Oakwood. He believes she is responsible. But she isn't.

—

Jill darts into the shadows behind the garage and waits. Her heart is pounding so hard it almost aches. She's clutching her lunch box. She is dying to move, but the many hours spying with Phoebe have taught her patience. Wait. Breathe. Watch.

What she's watching is Brian fiddling with the knobs on the barbecue as he tries to get the gas going. Jill is in the Murrays' backyard, behind the garage, ready. Her legs tremble with the exertion of standing still.

Brian moves towards the house, screen door slamming behind him. Jill knows they are having hamburgers for supper because she was here after school to take the baby for a walk in her stroller.

This is what Jill has become good at, pushing the baby stroller and reading stories to Kayla and Jamie when Laurel is busy in the kitchen. As she had been this afternoon, mixing bread crumbs and eggs into the hamburger meat, pounding out patties, placing the dozen small, round circles onto a plate covered with Saran Wrap, sliding the plate into the fridge. Laurel always makes burgers by the dozen, to match the buns, and microwaves the leftovers for the kids' lunch the next day.

Brian pushes open the screen door, balancing that plate in one hand, a beer in the other. He lines up the patties on the grill, shifting them with the spatula, pops the tab on his beer, and settles into his lawn chair. Jill waits.

"Laurel, do we have any barbecue sauce?" Brian calls into the house. A muffled answer comes through the back window.

"What?" Brain says, louder.

Laurel comes to the back door.

"I'm busy," she says through the screen. "We have some in the fridge. Come and get it."

Brian sighs, puts down his beer, heads back up the wooden stairs.

Jill is off like a shot across the yard. She grabs a meat patty from the barbecue and slides it into the lunch box. It is pink and raw, perfect. She keeps moving, back into the garage, crouches down in the corner with the rakes and ladder, heart slamming against her chest. She counts to ten slowly in her head. She peers around the garage door, sees Brian squeezing sauce onto the patties. He lifts the spatula, rearranges the position of the burgers, and does not notice one is missing.

Jill presses back into her corner, staring into the gloom, waiting for her eyes to adjust so she can pick out shapes. Her heart slows to a crawl, almost giving her a headache with its sudden sluggishness. The hamburger smell wafts over her and her stomach grumbles. Of course she did not eat any lunch today and for a second she's almost dizzy with the need to sit in the Murrays' backyard and eat a hamburger on a bun with sauce and pickles. She knows how to make this pass. She picks out one object in the garage, and stares at it steadily, without blinking—it is Kayla's bike—and then the swirling need recedes. Hunger can be pushed down, so far under it no longer exists. Jill has learned this.

Jill checks again, and it's time, Brian is in his lawn chair under the tree, sipping his beer, leaning over occasionally to flip the burgers.

Jill pounces onto the hood of the black car.

She stretches just a bit and her fingers reach the poison shelf. She pulls down the silver box that is exactly like the one the men used for the rats in her basement. She had watched those men closely and she had recognized the box immediately when she climbed up here on the ladder to get Laurel the weed killer that time.

Jill shakes the box, dribbles the white powder into her lunch pail, on top of the hamburger, then snaps the lid shut. Her arm goes up and returns the poison to its shelf. The box falls onto its side, but she can't waste any more time straightening what's crooked. She leaps off the car. She does not look back to see how a white patch of poison feathers down against the black hood of Brian's shiny car, leaving a faint outline of a girl's foot. Jill's footprint.

Jill is flying down the back lane, thin brown hair floating straight out behind her like a skinny tail. She is flying free and alive and so strong she could run forever.

She goes directly to the graveyard, to The Nest, and here she sinks to the ground. She has a stitch in her right side from running. She's panting, so she lies very still on her stomach, inhaling the rich earth, the grass, the worms.

Jill almost falls asleep.

The early evening sun is like lemon drops pressing on her closed eyelids, warming her nose. But then she sees the teeth, sharp in her mind, biting her wide awake. Jill sits up, pulls the lunch box to her, and opens it. The slurpy pink meat sickens her now. She holds her breath so she does not have to smell it.

Jill works quickly, as she had seen Laurel work this afternoon, mixing the meat and powder into balls. She has four little balls. She should have grabbed more meat. She puts the raw meatballs into her metal box and stands up.

Time to get out of here.

Jill walks past the Witch's house and the Warbanskis'. She can hear Fifi the poodle next door to them, yapping. Jill circles around back, to the fence.

"Fi-Fi-Fi-Fi," she sings through a knothole in the wood. Fifi's wet nose pokes through. Jill pushes the meatball inside and watches Fifi sniff, open her mouth, the teeth are chomping, chomping down. The moment the meatball leaves her hand Jill feels a giddy freedom, exactly as she felt facing Bea. She trembles with her power. She is stronger than her mother, braver than stupid Jill and quicker than the dogs with their menacing teeth.

Jill moves on, down the back lane.

At the teenager's house, where Tom lives, Baxter prowls the yard like a sentry. Here Jill tosses her treat over the fence, exactly like she and Phoebe toss rocks into the middle of this yard, and Baxter growls. He hunkers down and eats the meat instantly. It is Baxter's teeth that she sees most of all. She'll show him who's boss.

Jill knows that most dogs eat when their masters do. Since it's just before suppertime now, the animals are hungry.

Janice sees her coming. She is weeding her perennial flowerbed.

"Hi there, Jill," she says and straightens.

Jill stops dead in her tracks and holds her lunch pail tighter.

"What are you up to?" Janice asks. The girl looks ill, she thinks. Edgy.

"Nothing," Jill says. "Nothing much anyhow."

"How is your job at the Murrays going?"

"Fine," Jill says. She takes one step, two, away.

Janice takes a step forward. She cannot quite put her finger on this, but something is not right. She has the finely honed mother's instincts and right now, she would swear that Jill is in trouble.

"Is something wrong, Jill?" she asks.

Jill looks startled and her eyes quickly slide away. She half turns now.

"I gotta go, that's all," Jill says. "I haven't had supper yet. I mean, Delores is home and everything. I need to go. I mean, bye." She does not give Janice a chance to ask anything else. She turns and sprints down Glendale Avenue.

Janice stands and watches her go, eyes narrowed. She really does not want Phoebe around this kid anymore. The feeling is too strong to ignore.

Jill is heading back towards the Murrays, to the German shepherd next door that seems to grin at her every day when she's minding her own business, working in Laurel's yard. This is Gary's dog, Cody.

Brian and Laurel and the three kids are in the backyard, eating.

"Hi Jill," Laurel calls, when she sees her coming down the back lane.

"Hi," Jill answers.

"Want some Coke? We have extra hamburgers here if you haven't eaten," Laurel offers.

"No, thank you. My mother will be home soon." Jill says.

"Okay. Well, I'll see you tomorrow then?" Laurel says.

Jill nods, holding the handle of her lunch box tighter, inching away, down the back lane. She goes to the far side of Gary's house, where the Murrays cannot see her. She calls Cody. He knows Jill's voice and he does not even bark as he trots over. He takes the meatball directly from the palm of her hand, swallowing it in a single gulp.

One more.

Jill carries on down the back lane, intending to stop wherever she sees a dog. But she walks and walks and walks, three blocks, then four before she hears a bark. She has to get rid of this meatball. She walks into the stranger's backyard where the bark came from and places the last meatball carefully in the centre of the dog dish. The dog is barking inside. Jill never sees this one.

She is surprised to find how close she is to the beach now. Jill feels so light with her empty lunch box that she feels like skipping, but that would be stupid, so she doesn't. She walks to the beach. Some little kids are on the swings, with their parents pushing them. The river moves in that lazy way it has in the evening, waiting to be bathed in gold and pink so it can stretch and slink off to bed.

Jill goes down by the water and collects a pile of rocks. She fills her lunch box, then walks along the bank to the far end of the beach where the teenagers come on summer nights to neck behind the boulders.

She flings the lunch box into the river, watching the ring of ripples spread gently outwards as it sinks down.

Jill turns and walks home up the front street, not the back lane, undetected by the satellites inching over the roofs of Glendale Avenue.

—

# ABOUT THE AUTHOR

**D**iane Poulin was born and raised in Montreal and graduated from Concordia University. She moved to Winnipeg in her twenties and considers herself passionately prairie.

Diane's main occupation is journalism, and she spent ten years as a reporter, producer and director with CBC Radio in Winnipeg. She left to work for the Mayor of Winnipeg as political communicator managing the media.

Diane harbours a love for creative writing and even as a hard-boiled reporter could be caught scribbling poetry, which has been published in *CV2* and *Our Times* magazine. *No Safe House* is her first novel.

Diane Poulin was born and raised in Montreal and graduated from Concordia University. She moved to Winnipeg in her twenties and considers herself passionately prairie.